BEDDING THE BEDDING

A SENTIENT OBJECT ROMANCE

ANNARA LAYNE

Copyright © 2025 by Annara Layne

All rights reserved.

No part of this book may be reproduced in any form or by any electronic or mechanical means, including information storage and retrieval systems, without written permission from the author, except for the use of brief quotations in a book review.

No part of this book may be used to train generative artificial intelligence (AI) technologies, nor may it be fed into any AI model for any reason, including but not limited to: generating a summary of the book, using it as a prompt for AI art, or running it through an AI checker. No AI was used in the making of this book and the author does not consent to this book being introduced to AI models for any reason.

To silk sheets. Even when you're not sentient, you're always worth it.

A NOTE FOR READERS

Nikki, the main character of this book, has an ex-boyfriend who's heavily implied to be emotionally abusive. While this relationship is in the past, it is relevant to her emotional state, and there is an on-page interaction between them.

Please take care of yourself, and if you need to set this book aside either for a while or forever, know that I am proud of you for taking care of yourself.

If you come across any other content you think merits a mention here, feel free to reach out.

CHAPTER ONE

I screw my eyes shut tight, hoping that when I open them again, the stain slowly spreading across the ceiling will have disappeared. I mumble something close to a prayer—not an actual one, because I'm not sure I believe there's anything or anyone out there to hear it. But at this point I'll take any help I can get from any entities, real or not.

I crack an eye open, hoping that maybe if I don't look at the giant water mark too directly, I'll somehow be able to will it back out of existence.

Nope.

Still there.

I guess I can't really call it a slow spread, considering I'm watching it spread in real time. No time lapse needed; the creep of water—or whatever that liquid is—is more like a trot than an actual creep.

A canter, even.

The only saving grace is that it's not a full-on gallop. However, it *is* making me use horse comparisons, and I don't even like horses, so…

Fuck.

This is the last thing I need. Two days after being fired, I really can't deal with my house crumbling down around me, too.

But it isn't actually your house, is it? a little voice whispers in the back of my mind. *You've been living here rent free for months, you can't exactly be mad about finally having to leave your ex-boyfriend's house.*

I sigh.

It's been seven months since my (now-ex) boyfriend Nick and I broke up after more years together than I'd like to admit. Honestly, the "Oh my god, Nick and Nikki, what are the chances, that's soooo cute" comments were the least obnoxious thing about the relationship.

When he left without a word, I stayed in the house. A part of me always expected he'd come back—first to me, then at least to claim the house (which was rightfully his, left to him by his grandma when she died). But after seven months without a single word from him, the thought of leaving this house behind feels good, like I'm finally giving myself permission to let go of the final thing I have tying me to the man who was a part of my life for far longer than he should have been.

I put on a random playlist and start packing, grabbing my hamper and shoving everything I can into it. It'll have to serve as a box to cart my things to her car, since I want to get out of here as soon as possible. I'm worried if I take the time to run to the store for boxes or bins, I'll lose my nerve. After all, this place is free, and it's not like I know where I'll be going next.

I can stay in a hotel for a few days, and then...well, I'll figure something out. I always do.

It doesn't take long to dump all my meager belongings in the car, and I don't even have to work hard to get it all to fit. That's what happens when you sold all of your belongings to move in with your long-distance boyfriend, moving from one house to another until you finally got some stability after he inherited a house, only for him to break up with you and abandon you in his shitty house three months later.

I'm just glad I hadn't gotten around to buying a couch or painting the walls like we'd discussed. It would be so much harder to leave if I had actually invested time or money into making this place a home.

There's a wet splat from somewhere inside as I close the door to the house for the final time. I almost turn back to investigate before remembering I don't actually need to. It's no longer my problem. This is no longer my home.

I barely glance back at the house as I slip into the driver's seat of my beat-up old Toyota Corolla, feeling like a massive weight has been lifted from my shoulders.

The car groans as we start down the street, leaving the last rotten reminders of Nick behind us. I turn the radio to the Top 40 station, singing along to pop songs at the top of my lungs, and I'm very thankful for my luck as the station plays nothing but breakup and girl power songs. Yes, technically, the breakup is long over, but still. Moving out of his house counts.

By the time I pull up to the motel—the cheapest one I was able to find, I am newly unemployed, after all—my mood has lifted considerably.

Only for it to plummet again when I see the sign nailed across the front door.

It's closed.

Permanently Closed.

And I already paid online.

It should be easy enough to contest the charges with my credit card, but still. That's a couple hundred bucks I won't have access to for the next few days, at least. I pull up the website where I found this place, and my low phone battery glares at me from the top corner of the screen: 8%. No problem, I'll pick the next cheapest place, drive there, and throw my phone on the charger.

I warily eye the cigarette charger—my car is old enough it doesn't have a USB input. But the last time I tried to use my adaptor, it got so hot the plastic melted, and to make matters worse, my phone hadn't even charged.

I've never minded having a crappy car. It gets me where I need to go, never breaks down despite all the other issues (aside from the charging problem, the radio doesn't always work and, though the AC works great, for some reason there's no heat). But Nick used to grumble about it whenever he rode in this car, which was almost every day, considering this *"piece of shit car"* was the only one we had, between the two of us. I'd thought he couldn't afford one. I learned the day he left that he could.

I snap my attention back to the present moment. 7% charge and I still haven't picked a new place to stay tonight. I learned my lesson with this first place, so I drive over before booking. I can't afford to put another fake-out stay on my card.

Thankfully, the Vacancy light is lit up on their sign, and the man behind the desk gives me a friendly smile as I walk into the tiny lobby. He gets me checked in quickly with a room that, while certainly not nice, has no suspicious stains spreading quickly across the ceiling. Thank fuck. The first thing to go right today.

Not the first good thing, I remind myself, hauling my giant backpack over my shoulder and muscling my way past the sticking door into my home for the next two days. Other things must have gone right today.

I drop my bag onto the second bed and pull my gratitude journal out of it, then sink onto the bed I'll be sleeping in. It's the one I always choose: the one closer to the bathroom and farther from the door. Fewer obstacles in the middle of the night, and even though I know it's ridiculous, it kind of makes me feel like if someone were to somehow enter my room in the middle of the night, I'd be able to take those extra three seconds to figure out how to defend myself.

I flip the journal to the last entry and write today's date below it, ready to tally up all the things I'm grateful for today.

I started the practice my senior year of high school, when depression first sank its teeth into me and I finally convinced my parents (after way more begging than I should have had to do) to let me see a therapist. Honestly, what finally did it was the reminder that therapy would be cheaper than a hospital stay, and if I didn't see a therapist soon, the hospital was where I was headed.

Or worse.

My therapist had suggested I keep a list of all the good things that happened to me every day. "I'm not saying you should ignore the bad," she said, catching onto my obvious unease. Focusing on just the good stuff sounded an awful lot like toxic positivity to me. "But depression makes it easy to lose sight of the good, so I want you to write it down at least three good things every day. They can be as little as they need to be to hit the quota. Maybe the sun shone. Maybe there was an extra chicken nugget in your order. Joy can be small, but it's *there*, and right now you need a reminder of that."

It had helped.

Not enough, but it had helped.

Enough so that eight years later, I'm still writing down the little joys in my life. On days like today, I can really feel the difference it makes in my mindset.

1. The second motel had an opening AND was $15 a night cheaper if I booked in person, so I actually saved a little money by not booking ahead of time.

2. That song I can never remember the name of with the la-la-las came on the radio four times today.

3.

I pause, trying to come up with something, but it's hard.

Today was not a day where three good things are easy to identify. I have no job, no home, no friends. I'm living in a motel with no idea where I'll go after this or how I'll be able to afford it. The five thousand dollars I have in savings will go fast if I'm paying motel rates, and nobody will rent to me without proof of income. Having to move out of Nick's home—

Oh.

There it is.

Thing number three.

And it's an incredibly obvious one.

3. I no longer have any ties to Nick McNalty.

I slam the journal closed with a grin. It feels damn good to be free. Free of Nick, free of the house that for some reason always kind of smells like warm cheese and now has water stains spreading across the ceilings, free of the job I hated every second of.

I launch myself off the bed, grab a generic motel-white towel from the little alcove outside the bathroom, and crank the water in the shower, correctly assuming I'll need to give it time to get warm. $55 a night doesn't exactly buy you a place with a state-of-the-art water heater.

By the time steam rises from the shower, my spirits have lifted considerably. The water is deliciously hot (enough to scald, something my mother and Nick both chided me about whenever they got the chance) and the little bar of soap smells surprisingly good for such a crappy motel. I hum the song with the la-la-las, telling myself I'll finally actually learn its name this weekend, and take my time washing every inch of my body. I feel like a brand-new woman, so I should have the squeaky-clean, shiny skin to show for it.

After, I wrap my towel around my body and wipe the condensation from the mirror. The face that looks back at me is bright, slightly pink from the heat, and happier than I've seen myself look in a long time.

I check to make sure my phone is actually charging, relieved to see it's at 38%, and slip into my pajamas before crawling into bed. The first thing I did after walking in the door was crank the air-conditioning all the way down—what's the point of staying in a hotel (fine, motel) if you can't sleep in a room so cold you could grow icicles if you wanted to?—so I shiver as I snuggle under the covers with my still-damp hair.

It doesn't take long for me to drift into sleep, and it's mercifully dreamless. Thank god. After the hell of the past few days I expected nightmares about getting fired (again) or being alone forever, or even Nick showing back up and trying to win me back.

But no, I sleep through the night without a care in the world.

CHAPTER TWO

THE CONTINENTAL BREAKFAST consists of stale pastries, bananas that are slightly past their prime, and those individual cups of brand-name cereal that you only ever see at places like this. It's exactly what I needed, that little jolt of familiarity, even if the thing itself isn't actually all that good.

But it's solid, dependable.

Like I thought Nick was at one point.

Those days are long over.

A part of me wonders if I should text him to let him know I've left his house. Isn't there something about keeping the HVAC running in the summer so the house doesn't mold, or something? I've already picked up my phone by the time I remember that it's quite literally no longer my problem, and I owe that man nothing.

Besides, I called and texted him a lot in those first few weeks, and he never bothered to respond. There's no reason to think he will now, or that he'll even see my text. He probably has me blocked.

I do, however, call to cancel all of the utilities. Those are in my name, and there's no sense in paying for Wi-Fi or a gas connection for a place nobody's using, especially since I no longer have a job to fund the bills. If Nick shows up and wants those things, well, he can be a big boy and figure something out for himself for the first time in his life.

Once the calls are done, which takes way longer than it

should because all utility companies make the cancellation process as hard as humanly possible, I stretch out on the bed with my laptop open, scrolling through all of the real estate rental sites I can find. It doesn't take long to realize that everything on the market is way out of my budget—not that I'll even have a budget for much longer unless I get a job soon.

I switch tracks, scrolling through every job listing site I can think of, even the less official ones, like Craigslist and community forums. I'm not too fussy about what I do, as long as it brings in a paycheck. I've been a waitress, a nanny, a cashier, a valet...the list goes on. But it seems like nobody's hiring in this town, except for the kinds of jobs that require degrees I don't have and personal connections I could never hope to make.

My heart sinks. This is it, isn't it? The end of the road. I have no job or house and won't be able to find either. I'm probably weeks away from having to do the unthinkable: call my parents and beg them to take me in.

We haven't talked in years, not even a *happy birthday* text, and the thought of going back to them makes me so anxious my back locks up and my eye twitches. Still, I think they'd do it if I asked, and it would at least give me a roof over my head while I looked for a less soul-crushing option.

Something dawns on me, making me bolt upright.

There's nothing keeping me here, not anymore. I don't even like this town anyway. I should take this opportunity to leave. To find something better. If I'm considering leaving to go live with my parents, then I might as well leave to go somewhere I might have a shot at actually being happy.

I pull up the notes app on my phone and write a list of things I'm looking for in a town:

1. Small, the kind of place where everyone knows everyone. It doesn't have to be tiny, but maybe 50,000 people max?

2. Close to a big city (within an hour or so) so I can go there if I want.

3. Cute vibes.

4. Cheap, ideally.

5. Not here.

I throw that last one in just as a reminder that I really can leave if I want to.

And I very much want to.

With those criteria in mind, I look for a list of all the towns in the state that might fit the bill. I've always loved the thought of living in a small town, and whenever I've stopped in small towns on vacation I've always felt like I'm home. And small towns tend to be cheaper, so that's a plus.

Half an hour into my search, I find something that looks so perfect I'm almost afraid to hope. The town of Newport, which is ridiculously named considering there's no body of water anywhere nearby, is a few hours away. It's a town of 4,000 people, and there's an apartment available over an antique store. The owner of the store is renting it out for cheap to someone who's willing to work the register for her. And by cheap, I mean $200 a month plus utilities, which I can easily afford on the minimum wage she'll pay for the work.

I send her an email, then as soon as I hit send, I think better of it and look up the phone number of the store so I can call her. I don't want to risk someone else contacting her before she has a chance to see my email.

"Hello, you've reached Newport Antiques. " The voice on the other end of the line is old, soft, and slightly gravelly, and I immediately think of a kindly grandmother who bakes peanut butter cookies.

"Hi, my name is Nikki. I saw your listing for the apartment and cashier opportunity, and I was wondering if you're still looking for someone?"

"I am. Are you local?"

"No, but I'm looking for a change, and Newport looks like exactly the kind of place I'd like to live. I just sent you an email with my resume, and I'm happy to provide references for the housing." I wince. I don't have references. Thankfully, she doesn't seem to care.

"Oh, there's no need, dear. Let me take a quick look at your resume." The line goes quiet as she does just that, and then she asks why I left my most recent job.

"They went through some restructuring and my whole department got cut." It's technically true. She doesn't need to know that my whole department consisted of only me, or that the restructuring consisted of getting rid of me and the new hire who missed half his shifts. "I do have retail experience, and I love antiques."

"I'm looking for someone to start by Wednesday—we're closed on Tuesdays, so that's the start of our work week. I can give it another week at the most, but I do need to fill this position as quickly as possible."

"I can be there tomorrow." I wince at how eager I sound, but her voice brightens enough in her response that I think maybe it's not a bad thing I showed her just how badly I want this.

"Oh, really? That would really be wonderful. I think this is going to be a great fit, Nikki. I have a very good feeling about this."

So do I. This feels *right* in a way that nothing has in a very long time.

"Just give me a call when you get into town—or come into the shop itself—and I'll get you all set up with the keys. Here's my personal number."

We exchange a couple more pleasantries and then I hang up, kicking my feet. One more night at the hotel and then I'll check out in the morning and drive the three hours to Newport.

I spend the afternoon in the pool. Motel pools are hit-or-miss, but this is one of the good ones: there are only a few cracks in the concrete around the edges, and the water is clean. This place is clearly well cared for.

I float for what feels like hours. The water is clear and cool, and my tension melts away from my shoulders. I'm really doing it. I'm leaving this terrible town behind and moving somewhere purely because I want to, without a plan.

My parents' disapproval rings in my ears. They wanted me to go to college, even though that would have involved taking out huge loans I'd likely never be able to pay back, when I didn't even know what I wanted to study. Honestly, I hated school, and there's no reason to think college would have been any different.

Then they hated Nick. Which, fine, I'll give them that one. Things with him were good at first, but then he turned into exactly the person they thought he was all along. By the time things went to shit with him, my relationship with my parents had been over for years. Talking to them wouldn't have helped; it just would have given them ammunition for yet another lecture.

And I get it. It's not like striking out on my own got me far, just a series of jobs I mostly didn't like, half of which I was fired from for reasons outside of my control; a four-year relationship with a guy who turned out to be a total dick; and…that's it.

That's all I've gotten, just a string of shitty jobs and a shitty ex.

But this feels different. Like my life is finally going to turn around.

I stay in the pool until close to dinner time, enjoying being alone in the water until the gate clangs open and a group of men spills into the pool area. They're loud, all of them talking over each other, and their presence makes me tense. Something about them reminds me of Nick and his friends when I met him. The way they act like they're the only ones here, even though I got here first. The way they're all dressed in basically the same outfit, like they all shop at the same place. The way every single one of them lets their eyes linger on me until I get uncomfortable enough to leave the pool, forcing myself to move slowly so they don't see any of the fear I feel.

I get back to my room still dripping, because I didn't want to rub the towel on my body with them watching me. I order a pizza to be delivered to me and spend as little time as possible at my door. I don't think the men would hurt me, not really, but there's something about the sheer amount of attention they gave my body that's set me on edge, and I'd rather just avoid any chance of running into them again.

CHAPTER THREE

NEWPORT IS everything I hoped it would be.

The town itself is tiny, with a downtown that's only four square blocks. The main street is literally called Main Street, and it's the only one with traffic lights; all the others just have stop signs at the corners. The buildings are all old brick, with cutesy awnings, and most of them are only one or two stories tall. There is one singular three-story building, and it's the town hall, the bank, and the post office rolled into one.

Newport is the kind of place that would make the perfect backdrop for one of those sappy movies about the grouchy city girl who moves to the tiny town and complains about not being able to find an over-priced fancy latte, until the hot local guy (who either works with trees in some capacity or owns the one coffeeshop in town) makes her fall in love with the town—and him.

The kind of movie I won't publicly admit to loving, because it doesn't fit the tough image I've carefully crafted for myself. But I've maybe seen every single one ever made, by every company, even the obscure indie ones you can only find if you're on the right forums.

Newport Antiques is located right on Main Street, and I follow Gertie's instructions for parking. I almost miss the alley she tells me to turn into, but I see it at the last second and swing into it, holding my breath as I maneuver the car into the tight space, and exhaling in relief once I'm sure I won't scrape my car along the brick buildings that line the alley. It's wide enough that if I'd seen it in time instead of doing a frantic turn, I wouldn't be having this problem, so that's something, at least.

I inch along the space between the buildings to find the tiny lot that's just big enough for three cars. It's empty, so I park right in the middle and look up at the steps in front of me.

If I've counted the doors right, these steps should lead up to my new apartment.

Butterflies tingle in my stomach at the thought.

I'm home.

I walk back down the alley and around the side of the building.

Main street is quiet, with only a couple of people walking around. I guess it is the middle of the day on a Friday—most people will be at work, and in a town this size, the number of unemployed people and retirees can't be all that high.

I pull the door to the antiques shop open. A bell tinkles as I step into the airconditioned space, and an elderly woman looks up from behind the counter.

"Welcome to Newport Antiques." The woman smiles at me as though she's known me all my life and is thrilled to see me again. It should be disconcerting, but it's charming and way more comforting than I would have expected.

"Are you Gertie?"

"Yes, I am." She's everything I imagined when we spoke over the phone. The exact type of small-town elderly woman who bakes peanut butter cookies and takes everyone under her wing.

"I'm Nikki."

"Oh, Nikki!" She beams at me. "Welcome, welcome. I'm so glad you were able to make it today. I'll have you start on Wednesday, but this way you can get settled in and get to know some of the locals. It's not often we have a new face who's not a tourist, and let me tell you, people are going to want to meet you. I'm betting Wednesday—well, this whole first week, really—will see a boom in business. The ones who already know about you are excited to meet Newport's newest resident, and the rest will jump on the curiosity train soon enough."

Tears come to my eyes as she chuckles, and I have to turn away and pretend to examine something on one of the nearby shelves. It's small and metal and beyond that, I couldn't really tell you much about it.

I can't remember the last time anyone was excited to see me. Not my old boss or coworkers, not Nick, not the people I saw at the grocery store as we all did our weekly shopping. I know Gertie is my boss and landlord, but fuck if she isn't already the closest thing I've had to a friend in a very, very long time.

If she notices my misty eyes when I turn back to her, she doesn't say anything.

"Come on upstairs, I'll give you the key so you can let yourself into the place. My grandson and his girlfriend will be around later, and they'll be happy to help you carry your things up those steps. We're a friendly bunch here, if a bit too inquisitive for our own good. You're enough of a novelty that I'm sure you'll have no problem getting help with absolutely anything you need." She pauses, then winks at me. "By inquisitive, I do mean we're a bunch of nosy fuckers, pardon my French."

I laugh, surprised by the mouth on this woman. So much for the sweet little granny who bakes peanut butter cookies.

"Oh, by the way, do you have any dietary restrictions? I was going to make a batch of my famous peanut butter cookies for you, but so many people have allergies or intolerances, I didn't want to greet you with a plate full of poison! Peanuts and gluten both seem to be on thin ice these days."

I giggle, shocked at the sound coming out of me. "No, peanuts and gluten are both fine for me. Anything but apples."

"And see, my backup is a nice oat-based apple crumble." She studies me closely. "Apples, apples, apples. Okay, that information should be locked away in the old vault." She taps her temple. "Let's get you settled in."

She puts up one of those old-fashioned "be back soon" signs

and spins the arm on the little clock to reflect that she'll be back ten minutes from now. Then she leads me through the back door of the shop, into the tiny lot where I've parked my car. She slowly works her way up the stairs, and her hobbling makes it clear why she doesn't live in this apartment herself.

"There are three entrances to the store: the front door, the back door, and then the interior one that leads straight down from the apartment. I tend to keep that one bolted from the inside, on the apartment side, to make sure nobody can accidentally find their way up there, but of course, that's up to you. The apartment doors—the external one and the one through the shop—have their own keys, and those will work on the external shop doors, too, though the shop doors won't work for the apartment. Oh, look at that, I'm absolutely talking your ear off. I wrote it all down for you, too, so you won't forget."

I'm not sure what she saw on my face to make her think I was overwhelmed, but she was wrong.

Well.

I *am* overwhelmed, but in a good way. For the first time in a very long time, I feel like I'm right where I'm supposed to be.

She opens the door, and I gasp at the sight that greets me inside. I saw a couple of pictures online, but they absolutely did not do this place justice.

It's a studio apartment with exposed brick and woodwork inside, and huge windows overlooking the street. Natural light floods through the windows, bathing the room in a soft but bright light. It's open and airy and the kind of place that would have easily cost me at least a thousand dollars in my old town—which wasn't even a particularly expensive place to live.

"This place is only $200?" I blurt out. It's a studio, but there's absolutely enough space to turn it into a one-bedroom. Maybe even a two-bedroom, if you kept the bedrooms small.

"Seemed fair, since I can only pay minimum wage at the shop. Besides, I own the building outright, and I have no interest in being the kind of landlord who uses a property to extort the people living there. Your rent will cover all of the utilities and a portion of the property tax—"

"Wait," I say, not even caring that I'm cutting her off. "Utilities are included?" I'd just assumed I'd have to pay for those on top of the rent. And that they'd be higher than I'm used to, since the town is so small. Cost of living in small towns is often lower, but there are certain things that do tend to cost more than their big-city counterparts, like utilities and groceries.

She smiles at my dumbfounded expression. "They sure are included. I'll show you around and then let you settle in."

An hour later I know all about the quirky shower and the thermostat that doesn't always show the correct temperature but does actually work well aside from that. I've brought the bare essentials up from my car and taken a shower, and now I'm lying on the bed, which was the last thing Gertie showed me before heading downstairs to tend to the shop.

"I initially purchased these sheets for the store," Gertie had told me, "but then I realized they'd go beautifully in here and I couldn't bring myself to give them up. They're new, never been slept in," she said, showing me the sheets, which are beautiful enough that I'd have had a hard time parting with them, too.

The duvet is a soft apricot color, and when she folded it down to expose the sheets, I noticed that they have subtle pink swirls only a couple shades off from the background color. The stitching at the top of the sheets is pale green, and sprays of embroidered flowers decorate the border. They're absolutely gorgeous, and easily the most expensive bedding I've ever encountered in my entire life.

"Well, I'm sure they were slept in at some point," she corrects herself. "They're antiques, after all; who knows how many people slept in them before they came into my possession. But they're new to this space, and they haven't been slept in since they changed hands. They've been well-washed, of course. If you'd rather not sleep on second-hand sheets, there are some new ones—*actually* new ones, bought just for your arrival—in the linen closet, just here."

I don't mind. I slept in a motel last night; I'm not about to be upset about pre-used sheets that are in good condition and clearly recently washed. And now that I'm lying on them, it turns out they're silk, and the satin weave is luxurious against my skin.

I close my eyes, relishing in the feeling.

And promptly burst into tears.

I'm home.

For the first time in as long as I can remember, I am actually somewhere that feels like home.

CHAPTER FOUR

I WAKE up to the sound of knocking on the door, and it takes a second for me to remember where I am: Newport, above the antique store, in my new home.

I stretch with a smile and notice that the light streaming through the windows is softer, like dusk is falling. I didn't mean to fall asleep, but it looks like I managed to nap for a few hours.

I pad over to the door and throw it open, belatedly realizing that I should probably ask who's on the other side before doing so. Not that I think anyone would want to hurt me. I have no enemies, and Newport doesn't seem like the kind of place where people knock on your door to try to kill you. But still.

The man on the other side of the door looks to be in his mid-twenties, with a heart-stopping smile and brown hair that swoops over one eye. He looks like something out of a romance novel, but maybe one written in the early 2000s. If I hadn't sworn off of romance after the whole Nick thing, I'd probably be swooning a bit at the sight of him.

"You must be Nikki," he says, flashing his perfect teeth at me and extending a hand for me to shake. "I'm Gertie's grandson, Jack. And this is my girlfriend, Eva." He steps aside to reveal a woman with model-good looks. She's tall and curvy, with black hair that cascades in waves down to her hips and striking green eyes. She gives me a soft smile and my heart stutters. She has the kind of looks that make me wonder if I really am straight, after all.

"It's so nice to meet you," she says in a melodious voice.

"Gertie asked us to stop by and see if you need any help unpacking."

"Oh, that's so nice. Sure, let me grab my keys."

It doesn't take us long to bring everything upstairs, where I fend off their offer to help me put all my things away. Just bringing everything up here was enough, and it's not like it'll take me long to unpack my meagre belongings on my own.

"Do you have dinner plans?" Eva asks. "Jack and I were thinking we'd go out for pizza, and we'd love to have you join us."

Pizza sounds great, as does the idea of making new friends, so I grab a dress and quickly change in the bathroom so I'm not showing up to my first outing in town in wrinkled clothes, then follow them to the Italian restaurant that's across the street and two doors down from my new home.

This might be the best pizza I've ever had, and it's half the price of anything back home. *Of anything in my old town,* I remind myself. Newport is home now.

I grin at the thought, and Eva grins back.

By the end of the meal, I'm stuffed and happy and have Eva's and Jack's numbers saved in my phone. We walk around downtown afterward, stopping at the ice cream parlor to get cones to eat while we walk, and a part of me is thrilled to see how quiet it is, given that it's a Friday night. There are people out and about, but not many. Jack and Eva introduce me to a handful of people, who all look at me with interest. Gertie wasn't kidding when she said that the new girl would pique everyone's interest.

By the time we part ways, I'm certain I made the right choice in moving here, and I'm looking forward to settling in. It's exactly the kind of small town I've always dreamed of living in.

I climb the steps to my apartment and lock the door behind me, then kick off my shoes and shimmy out of my dress before I realize the curtains are still open. I dash over to them and yank them closed, but thankfully it looks like nobody's on the street below. It is 11:00 pm in a town with only three stoplights downtown, after all. I guess I shouldn't be surprised there's nobody out at this late hour.

I bet there's probably one singular bar in town, and that that's where everyone who's still awake and out of the house is. I make a mental note to look it up—or ask someone where it is—so I can check it out next weekend.

I take another quick shower and slip into the oversized shirt and threadbare shorts that have become my default pajamas because they're just so damn comfortable.

I'm not sure if it's the move, or the late night out with my new friends, or these absolutely delectable sheets that Gertie provided me, but I fall asleep almost the moment I turn the light off.

Unlike last night, I have dreams.

And holy shit, the dreams...

I wake up in the morning panting and absolutely drenched.

In sweat, yes, but also between my legs.

I don't remember all of the details. In fact, I don't remember *most* of the details.

All I remember is flashes of touch, of soft fingers trailing down my body. Of me moaning and arching into the sensation, and those fingers dipping between my legs, so soft, almost a silky touch.

Judging by the light peeking around the edges of the curtains, it's early—like, way earlier than I would ever get up unless I was forced to, but I'm way too turned on to go back to sleep.

The soft morning sunlight peeks through my curtains, leaving a stripe of light right across the part of me that's slick and throbbing with desire, and I slide a hand between my legs to take care of the desperate need there.

My fingers slide across my clit, lubed up from the intensity of that dream. It's almost obscene how wet I am—I'm not sure I'll have enough friction to be able to do what I need to do.

I wish I could remember anything about the man in my

dream. The way I feel now, like my body is on fire in the most delicious way, is like nothing I've ever felt before. Even in the early days with Nick, back when we'd find any excuse we could to sneak away to a bathroom or a backseat or anywhere we could be alone—or even just mostly alone—he *never* made me feel like I would combust if I didn't get his hands on me. But that dream...

It takes seconds for me to tumble over the edge. Normally I need penetration *and* something working my clit in order to come, but a few quick glides of my hand across that bundle of nerves and my back is arching off the bed and I let out a guttural scream that's unlike any sound I've ever made before.

I freeze, worried that I was too loud, and that they'll be able to hear me downstairs in the shop, but when I glance over at the alarm clock, it turns out it's only 6 am. Thank god; I don't need my new landlord-slash-boss to think I'm getting murdered up here, when I'm really just...frustrated. Sexually speaking.

That would be so humiliating.

I drag myself out of bed and take a quick shower to wash away the evidence of the hottest dream I've ever had.

When I get back to bed, the sheets, which I expected to be soaked with my arousal, are perfectly dry.

Huh.

I guess my legs were closed until I woke up. There was definitely enough slickness on my thighs to account for it all.

I throw on a pair of jeans and a cute top and make my way to the diner next door, pleased with how close everything is in this little town. Even on the days I can't be bothered to actually get up and make an effort, I'll be able to drag myself one door over to pick up food.

The girl behind the counter looks young, maybe high-school-aged, and she greets me with a sunny smile.

"You're Nikki, right?"

I grin. "Word spreads fast here, huh?"

"I'm Anya. Eva's my aunt. She said she was hanging out with you yesterday."

"Oh, yeah. She's great."

"Yeah. What do you want? And are you, like, a regular order kind of person, or someone who gets something different every day?"

"Uhhhh..."

"I'm just asking because if you have a regular order, I can make sure it's ready for you by the time you come in, but if you get something different each time, I'll wait."

"Oh, I'm not sure I'll be getting coffee from here regularly. That can get expensive."

"Only for tourists." Anya shrugs. "Locals get black coffee for a dollar, something fancy for three, and something in the middle for two."

Oh damn. For those prices, maybe I *will* get coffee here every day.

A thought I clearly say aloud, because Anya laughs. "Yeah, I thought that's what you'd say. So?"

"I need a second with the menu."

It doesn't take long for me to settle on my order: a cinnamon mocha with a day-old surprise pastry, which only costs a dollar. Apparently the option is to sell them for cheap, throw them away, or donate them. Anya tells me there aren't always day-old pastries available, it all depends on what didn't sell the day before. But usually there are at least a few left over at breakfast-time.

"If you have any allergies or if there's anything you really hate, just tell us and we'll make sure your pastry doesn't contain that ingredient."

"I'm allergic to apples."

Anya snorts. I open my mouth to defend myself, but she hurries to explain before I can get the words out. "Sorry, it's just with your pale skin and short black hair you kind of look like Snow White, so that'll be easy to remember."

I've never thought of that before, but she has a point. Maybe I'll start making that comparison myself, to help people remember.

"That'll be four dollars."

I hand her my card and she lets me know that, even though everywhere takes cards in Newport, most businesses prefer cash.

Of course they do. That's exactly the kind of quaint thing I should expect from a town this size. I haven't carried cash in years, but I'll be sure to run by the ATM and start keeping some on me for my breakfast and whatever else I decide to buy every day.

I still can't believe that for three or four dollars a day, I'll get a coffee and a pastry. And I barely have to leave my house to get them.

Moving to Newport was the best decision of my entire life.

I take a sip of my mocha and my eyes roll back in my head. "Okay, yeah, I want one of these every day. Please."

"You got it. Same time?"

I shake my head. "I'll let you know once I have my work schedule, but I usually sleep in on weekends. So, let's do weekdays only, and on weekends maybe I'll try something new."

"Sounds good."

"Wait, isn't this place supposed to be a diner?" I ask, suddenly realizing that with the couches, plush chairs, and low tables scattered around the room, this feels more like a coffee shop.

Anya shrugs. "Small town. It's both. The diner is technically next door, but you can get there through that hallway." She points to an archway off to the far side of the room. "It's owned by the same people and most of the workers are trained for both sides. Over here is mostly coffee, tea, and pastries, and over there is the more diner-y stuff like eggs and hash browns and bacon. There's a spinach quiche that's apparently really good, if you like spinach. I don't, so I can't actually recommend it." She laughs.

I make a mental note to come to the diner for breakfast tomorrow, and Anya lets me know there's a separate entrance for it one door down. "You can get there from in here, but that door will take you straight to the diner."

I thank her and head outside, taking another sip of my mocha and clutching my raspberry scone in my hand, ready to explore the town that's going to be my home for the foreseeable future.

CHAPTER FIVE

FOR SUCH A SMALL TOWN, especially one that was so quiet on a Friday night, there sure are a shitload of people downtown on Saturday morning. I should know—every single one of them introduce themselves to me. The quiet last night made me think it would be hard to make new friends, but today is proving that the absence of a nightlife doesn't necessarily mean an absence of *people*. I guess Saturday is the day the whole town is out and about.

By lunchtime, I have fifteen new numbers saved in my phone, and I've somehow agreed to get lunch with a group of women who I think make up the local gardening group but honestly, it's all a bit of a blur. I join them at The Club, which is a sandwich place one street over from where I live.

The women in the gardening group are all around my age, which surprised me at first, but I guess gardening isn't just a hobby for old people. I don't have a yard at my apartment, but I bet I could grow some flowers in window boxes, or something. The gardening club will help me figure it out.

"We were all so thrilled when we heard Gertie found someone to work at the store. She's been doing it all herself since George left, and it's been taking its toll on her. She's tough, but she's getting up there in years," a blonde woman who I think is named Susan says. Or maybe it's Suzie.

Susannah?

"What brought you to Newport?" another one of the women asks. This one has strawberry blonde hair and deep plum lipstick that shouldn't work with her complexion nearly as well as it does. I think her name is Lauren, or Laurie. Honestly, it could be Kate. There are so many of them it's hard to keep them all straight.

"I just needed a change. I've always wanted to live in a small town, and my old job did some restructuring, so I was no longer needed." A sea of sympathetic faces wince back at me. "And I'd been living at my ex-boyfriend's house, so I figured, there was no reason to stay."

"I could never live with a man after we broke up," Jezelle says. I actually remember her name, partly because it's so unusual, and partly because it rhymes with gazelle, which she kind of looks like, with her long face and sleek cheekbones.

"Oh, he wasn't there anymore. He moved out when—when we broke up." I stumble over the words a bit, because the over-simplification almost feels like a lie. But they don't need my whole sob story. "I stayed because it was free, but..." I shrug.

"Oh, in that case, I could never have moved away." Jezelle laughs, but there's none of the malice I might have expected from such seemingly passive aggressive words, especially coming from a woman as gorgeous as her. She looks like she could have been head mean girl in high school. But I'm not getting those vibes from her, and I feel guilty for thinking it.

Honestly, I'm the last person who should be judging anyone.

Hazel is the only one at the table who might actually be a mean girl. She hasn't said a single word to me beyond her own name, and she keeps shooting glances my way that I can't quite interpret. She's either a colossal bitch or painfully shy, and I honestly have no idea which it is.

The rest of the meal passes quickly, and I realize how easy it's been to talk to these strangers. They all put their numbers into my phone (even Hazel, at Jezelle's insistence), and Jezelle adds me to their group chat.

The Garden Gals.

"It's code," she says with a wink, texting "This is Jezelle.

Welcome to the club, Nikki." with a maple leaf and a smoke emoji after my name.

Oh.

We've never even talked about drugs, but the fact that they just assumed I'd be down feels better than it probably should. Because yeah, I am.

We all hug goodbye and I wander around some more, stopping into most of the shops I didn't hit this morning.

My feet are aching by the time I drag myself up the stairs to my apartment, with a pizza and garlic bread in hand. I've never eaten so much pizza in my life, but hey, it's quick and easy and at least contains some vegetables.

I drop into one of the plush chairs in the living area and eat, scrolling through my emails on my phone. I pause at one that's eight down.

It's from Nick.

My breath hitches.

I'm not sure why.

Sure, things didn't exactly end well between us, if you can even call him just up and disappearing an ending. But it's not like I have any emotional attachment to him anymore, and it's not like I'm scared of him or anything.

So why is my heart racing?

Maybe because I haven't heard from him in seven months, and now he's contacting me three days after I moved out. Is it just a coincidence that he found out so quickly, or did he know the moment I moved out? And if so, how?

My fingers shake as I open the email, and his words prove that I was right to be on my guard.

Where the fuck are you? The utilities have all been turned off, were you planning on telling me or just running away like you always fucking do? I can't believe you'd be so fucking irresponsible and imma-ture. You owe me back rent for all the time you lived at my house for free.

He can't actually charge me back rent, considering we never

had a lease or even an agreement of any kind. I looked it up when he first left and I was deciding whether I would stay in the house or not. But I know he'll try to collect if he can.

Once he sets his mind to something, Nick won't give up until he gets it.

But I won't give in. Not this time. There's nothing he can do to convince me that I should pay him for the privilege of being ghosted.

I ignore his email.

I owe him nothing.

I chant the words on repeat in my mind. *I owe him nothing, I owe him nothing, I owe him nothing.*

By the time I crawl into bed, I almost believe it. I expect a sleepless night, but I fall asleep almost instantly.

I wake up in the morning wet again, but just like last night I don't remember my dreams. I just know my clit is throbbing and my nipples are aching, and I feel like I'm going to explode if I don't come as soon as possible.

The shower has a handheld attachment with strong water pressure, and I decide to test that out. Steam rises around me from the main shower head as I aim the attachment at my nipple, gasping as the blast of water hits the sensitive peak.

I alternate between my nipples until I can't take it anymore and aim the stream of hot water at my clit. I slide my other fingers inside myself and pump hard and fast. Within seconds I'm gasping and curling my toes as my orgasm rocks through me.

By the time I step out of the shower I'm feeling refreshed and ready for my last day of exploring before I start work at the antique store. I don't know what to expect: is this the kind of small town where everything is closed on Sundays, or can I check out the few stores I didn't go into yesterday?

I slip into my favorite sundress and head outside to find out.

I don't make it far before Jezelle calls my name and invites me over to garden with the group. "We'll actually be gardening," she says

"I don't have any experience with actual gardening, but I'd love to join."

"If it helps, we'll be high, too."

I laugh. "Now that, I have experience with."

I run upstairs and change into a pair of jeans shorts and an old t-shirt I don't care about, because I don't want to risk ruining my favorite dress. When I get back down to Main Street, Jezelle is waiting for me with a cinnamon mocha and a day-old chocolate croissant. Gotta love small towns.

We stroll over to her house, which is about four blocks out of the downtown area, and I gasp at the sight of her garden.

Colorful flowers spill over her wooden fence, in all shades of red, pink, purple, yellow, orange, white—and even blue, which I've never seen before. It's the kind of wild garden that's technically overgrown, but you'd never actually call it that, because it looks amazing. Like an explosion of wildflowers right here on this residential street.

"Jezelle, this is amazing."

"It's my pride and joy. Come on, we're working in the backyard today. We rotate houses each week, and I know you don't have a garden in your apartment, but if you ever want our help with houseplants or if you want to apply for a plot in the community garden, just let us know and we'll be happy to help you."

It's the perfect day, even if I do have to put up with Hazel glaring at me whenever she catches me looking her way.

I get way higher than I intend to, and Jezelle offers me her spare room once it becomes apparent that I am definitely not capable of walking the few blocks back to my apartment. One of the girls offers to drive me, but the room is spinning a bit and I'm so tired I face plant into the bed the moment Jezelle leads me to the room.

I blame the bong rips.

I wake up in a bed that isn't mine, and my first thought isn't to wonder where I am, or whether I might have made a bad impression on my new friends last night.

My first thought is that, for the first time since I came to Newport, I haven't had any sexy dreams.

My second thought is that I miss them.

Not just the dreams, either. I miss the sheets.

The ones at Jezelle's are comfortable. They're soft and a pretty shade of pale blue, and they're just lovely overall.

But they're not *my* sheets.

It's ridiculous. I've only slept in my sheets twice; I don't know why I already have such a strong attachment to them.

The smell of coffee and bacon inspires me to get up, and I join Jezelle at her table. She's already dressed for the day, but I'm still in my clothes from last night.

"I did not mean to get that high," I mumble as I drop into the seat across from her.

"It happens to the best of us," Jezelle snorts. "Now come on, let's get some food into you."

I spend the next two days at home, partially hiding from the world after the humiliation of being the one girl who couldn't handle her pot, and partially because I want to settle into the apartment so it can really start to feel like home.

By the time Wednesday rolls around I'm excited for my first week of work. I arrive for my shift five minutes early with two coffees in hand: my cinnamon mocha and the plain black coffee (no milk *and* no sugar) that Anya assured me is Gertie's favorite.

The way my boss's eyes light up when I hand it to her confirms the young barista was right.

"You're early," Gertie says approvingly.

"I try to be. Plus, it's easy, considering I literally live at work."

Gertie chuckles and takes a sip of her coffee, then sets it on the counter. "This week, you and I will work together. I'll show you everything you need to know, and next week you'll have your first solo shift."

We jump right in. She shows me how to use the register, which I get a lot of practice with: even though it felt like I'd met the whole town over the weekend, there's a steady stream of customers wanting to lay eyes on me for the first time, or meet me again, or just show their support.

I'm not used to being the center of attention like this, but I find that I don't mind it. I'm sure it'll slow down soon, anyway. By the end of the day Sunday, the Garden Gals were already treating me like I'd always been one of them, and I bet my novelty will wear off for the rest of the town soon, too.

"I usually close the shop for a half hour for lunch. In peak tourist season—that's autumn, when people come through here when they're visiting nearby towns to see the leaves changing— I sometimes end up skipping lunch. I don't expect you to do that, but if you ever do work through lunch, you just let me know and I'll give you an extra half hour's pay to make up for it."

She notices my confused expression.

"I don't do all that clocking in and out nonsense. You'll be paid for the hours on the schedule, open to close plus a fifteen-minute buffer on either end. Your time is your time, and I trust you've got a good head on your shoulders, so if you need to close for a few minutes here and there, just do it. The beauty of a small town is that we have the freedom to be flexible with our hours rather than being beholden to a corporate schedule. But I've based the pay on an assumption that you'll take a half hour break in the middle of your day, so if you don't, I'll need to adjust your pay to reflect that. It's only fair."

Wow.

I can't imagine my old boss doing something like this. In fact, he regularly made me work through my legally mandated lunch break, but forced me to clock out even though I was still doing the work. He made it very clear he would fire me if I took my break or reported him to the labor board, and while the law would have been on my side, I still would have lost a paycheck that I desperately needed, so I put up with it, until he ended up firing me anyway.

I never could have imagined going from that job and that housing situation to what I have now.

Since there are two of us working every day this week, we won't be closing the store for lunch. Gertie gives me a full half-hour break to eat in the back room, but when it's her turn for lunch she stays at the counter so I'm not completely alone, which I appreciate. Especially when the register gets stuck and she has to help me fix it.

"This is only the second time that's happened, so I don't think it's time to replace it just yet, but you keep an eye on that and let me know if it becomes a problem," she says, jimmying the cash drawer open.

She shows me all the other little quirks of the place, and by the time we close I feel like I have a good handle on things—and I've probably met another hundred Newport residents, at least.

She leaves through the front door and watches me lock up behind her before I head upstairs. It's not exactly the most exciting job in the world, but it's easy, I get to talk to people and sell some really cool antiques, and it brought me to a place I could really see living for the rest of my life.

I drift into sleep content with how my first day went, and the whole rest of the week follows in the same easy way.

On Monday night, which is essentially my Friday, I stay up late having a solo movie marathon. All of them feature people moving to towns the size of Newport and falling in love, and I start to think that maybe, in a few months, I might be open to the possibility. Not yet, but it would be nice to have someone. Every morning since I got here, I've woken up wet from dreams I don't remember, and it would be nice to have someone help me take care of the ache between my legs.

"Just because you want to get fucked doesn't mean you want a relationship, Nikki," I remind myself out loud as I get ready for bed. "I just need to get fucked, that's all. Soon."

I think about getting my toys out for a quick masturbation session, but it's late, and I'm tired, and there's a part of me that wants actual sex, like, with a partner, so badly that I'm not sure my own attempts will cut it tonight.

I drift off to sleep already tense, so it shouldn't come as a surprise when I wake up in the middle of the night, too turned on to go back to sleep.

CHAPTER SIX

My hand is already between my legs when I wake up, rubbing against the wet patch in my panties.

I roll over, trying to will myself back to sleep, but my whole body is taut and the feeling of the soft, silky sheets against my skin causes me to groan. Even though I'm the one who made the sound, it sends a bolt of heat directly to my core.

What is it about Newport that makes me so fucking horny in my sleep?

Maybe it's just the fact that I've left my boring, dead-end job and a town I never really felt like I belonged in. I might just be reacting to my newfound freedom and the feeling of safety and stability that comes with it.

I must move unconsciously while I'm thinking about it, because I feel the sheets sliding against my skin, and my core tightens.

Okay, so until I've adjusted to this new period in my life, I guess I just have to masturbate every night and/or morning. I can do that.

I laugh aloud, and the sound of it is loud in the otherwise silent night.

This isn't exactly a problem I ever thought I'd have, but then again...it isn't exactly a problem at all.

This morning—or yesterday morning, I guess, considering it's now 2:00 AM—I woke up so turned on from my dream that it didn't take long to get myself off. But tonight, I'm going to take my time with it.

I grab my pleasure bag from my bedside table and pull out my favorite dildo. It's purple, and girthy, with thick veins that stick out enough that you can really feel them as it slides in and out.

I set my vibrator on the pillow next to me for when I'm ready. I like to get myself as close as possible with penetration alone and then bring in the vibrator to get me the rest of the way there.

Or the other way around sometimes, when I'm feeling extra spicy.

"God, I need to be fucked," I groan as I notch the dildo at my entrance and spread my legs to get a better angle, but I must have tangled the sheets up more than I thought earlier, because one of my ankles gets caught, and I can't quite free it.

And look, I've watched my fair share of light bondage porn, but I don't exactly want my first time to be an accidental solo case.

I kick my leg, trying to free it, but that only seems to make things worse.

I drop the dildo and sit upright, grabbing the sheet around the ankle and trying to work it loose so I can slide my leg out.

Except the sheet doesn't budge.

In fact, it somehow gets tighter.

I turn the light on so I can get a better look at the situation and see how I managed to get so thoroughly tangled up in my sheets.

Everything looks normal. There's no knot or anything, just sheets that have gotten twisted around themselves, and my ankle, over and over.

I have no idea how I managed to get so tangled.

What I do know is that I should be confused, maybe a little scared. There's nobody here to free me, after all. And what if I'd gotten tied up somewhere else, like around my neck?

But I'm not confused or scared. I'm...turned on.

The sheets are so silky, and the feeling of being trapped here, even if there's nobody else to do anything to me, is hot as hell.

I give up on trying to free myself and turn my light back off. I've always loved how much more intensely you can feel things in the dark.

I grab my dildo, rubbing it along my clit.

But when I go to pinch my nipple with my other hand, I find that wrist trapped, too.

The fitted sheet has come up and rolled itself over my hand. And then somehow gotten tucked back in under my mattress?

It makes no sense.

But frankly, I'm way too turned on to care.

I buck against the dildo, ready to finally feel it sink inside me.

And then my sheets unmistakably move.

There's a slide of silk satin against the ankle that's still free. And then another against the hand that's holding the dildo, quickly pinning it up next to my head. I drop the dildo as my hand flies upward. Just like that, all four of my limbs are strapped to my bed with a caress of silk.

Finally, it clicks.

I'm dreaming.

I must be.

And holy hell, I understand why I woke up so wet yesterday.

Except this feels different from the dreams I've been having. Those have been hazy and nonspecific, erotic but without any actual details. This feels like real life—I've never felt this awake during a dream before.

Why am I examining this so hard? I close my eyes and give into the sensation as the softness of the sheets, the coziness of the blanket, and the wetness between my leg combine into the most delicious combination of sensuality.

But it's not enough to get me off. Not yet. I writhe, desperately trying to rock against the dildo that lies just an inch or two away from where I need it to be.

I feel the slide of silicone against my slick core when I move just right, but I can't get it inside me.

I whine, so desperate and needy, but I can't quite reach the pleasure I'm so desperate for.

Suddenly, understanding dawns. This is why I was so wound up when I woke up. I'd been dreaming of being edged. I bet this went on for hours in dream time. It wasn't just a sexy dream; it was a dream designed to turn me on and get me as close to the edge as possible—and then keep me there indefinitely.

But still, there's that voice in my mind that whispers that this is different. That those were just dreams, and this is something more.

But it can't be.

I'm panting, bucking my hips, whimpering and begging to be allowed to get off. To be fucked by my dildo.

To be fucked by my sheets.

It's so absurd it should turn me off, but honestly who knows how dream logic works. It's fine.

I close my eyes, letting the sensations overtake me. If I'm going to have a hyper-realistic sex dream about my sheets, I'm damn well going to enjoy it.

The silk tightens against my wrists and ankles for a second before loosening slightly, almost like the sheets are showing their approval at my surrender.

Which, yeah, is super fucking hot.

"Fuck," I moan, fighting against the instinct to try to press my thighs together so I can at least get some friction there. A moment later, I'm rewarded for my restraint with a brush of silk against my aching, throbbing clit.

My back bows off the bed and I let out a sound halfway between a gasp and a moan. If I thought the sound I made earlier was hot, it had nothing on this. It's *filthy*, and the satiny silk seems to react to it, pressing harder against me. The sheets twist, pinching my clit between them, and I scream in response, not caring about how loud I'm being. The neighbors are probably all asleep.

Besides, *I'm* (probably) asleep. I'm dreaming. I *must* be. My certainty is faltering the longer this incredibly erotic dream goes on, but I'm too addled with lust to think about what it would mean if I actually am awake. For now, we're going with this being a dream, and I'm probably not making any sounds out there in the real world.

Here in my dream, though? I'm moaning and gasping and begging for more, which my sheets readily give me.

Silk glides along my skin in a tantalizing tease, like it's gently promising me that it will make me feel good if I just let it.

I bite my lip, remembering how the sheets responded to my restraint last time. Maybe if I'm quiet, they'll fuck me harder.

A moment later, I'm rewarded for it.

The pressure on my clit heightens, and I swallow my cries as my pleasure skyrockets.

The sheet rubs against my clit, maintaining a deep, steady pressure, until I'm silently sobbing with need. For someone else, this might be enough to produce an orgasm, but I can't come unless I have *both* internal and external stimulation. The other night was a fluke, and one that's clearly not about to happen again.

"Please," I whisper. "I need you inside me. *Please.*" My voice breaks on the final plea and that seems to spur the sheets on. The fitted sheet tightens its hold on my wrists, and I feel silk brush the insides of my thighs in a twisting motion. As though the top sheet is fashioning itself into a shape that could penetrate me better.

And then, sweet Jesus, it does.

In one fast motion, a thick rope of silk thrusts into me. I'm so wet it slides in without resistance, and I whimper at the feeling of it. I've never felt so full from a partner before, and it's fucking delicious.

Even though this isn't even really a partner, a voice at the back of my mind whispers. *Even though this isn't even* real.

The silk phallus inside me pauses, like its waiting for something, and without thinking the words "thank you" fall from my lips.

As if in response, it pulls out slowly, then slams back into me. The intrusion is very, *very* welcome.

I want to pinch my nipples. I want to play with my clit. I want to do so many things, and the fact that I can't do any of them because of the restraints is so tantalizing.

The top sheet keeps fucking in and out of me, making my toes curl as it drags against my g-spot, making me see stars.

But since it's only inside me now, and not playing with my clit anyone, I still can't quite get there.

"I need you to play with my clit, too," I moan. "Please, that's the only way I can get off. I need both, at the same time."

Talking to my sheets like this, telling them how I need to be fucked, should feel ridiculous, but it doesn't. Especially once they apply pressure exactly where I need it, and I can feel that elusive pressure coiling low down in my belly.

This is the point where partners often fuck it up. They change their pattern, or start talking dirty to me, saying a lot of really unsexy stuff that makes my orgasm disappear right as it's about to happen. But the thing about sheets is they can't talk, and they don't have their own orgasm to distract them from focusing on mine.

They keep up a steady pace, drawing me closer and closer to my release.

I scream when it finally hits me, wave after wave of pleasure coursing through me. My toes go numb. I literally see stars. My pussy pulses, drenching the sheets in my come, and holy shit am I squirting? I've never done that before. Fuck this feels so good.

Through it all, the sheets keep going, pinning me to the bed, thrusting in and out of me, pinching my clit over and over, guiding me through the most intense orgasm I have ever had in my life.

When the flood finally stops, the sheet gently withdraws from inside me, soft satin gliding across my sensitive skin.

My wrists and ankles are freed, but it takes a few minutes before I can move. I am utterly wrecked, worn out and thoroughly satisfied, and the final thought I have before drifting off to sleep in a puddle of my own explosive come is that this experience, this bizarre too-real dream, has ruined me for anyone else. I have been so thoroughly fucked by these vintage sheets that the thought of letting anyone else even try to make me feel like this feels laughable.

As I sink into sleep, I swear my sheets caress me in satisfaction.

CHAPTER SEVEN

I WAKE up on Tuesday to sun streaming through my windows. My whole body is deliciously sore, like it sometimes gets a few days after going on a strenuous hike.

The events of last night come back to me in a flash. Instead of the vague memories and feelings I've been waking up with, I remember every last detail of my bedding fucking me.

The way my sheets restrained me to the bed. The way they teased me.

The way they pulled the most intense orgasm of my life out of me.

I stretch, luxuriating in the late morning light. It's my final day before I start work, and I'm torn between snuggling deeper under the covers or getting up to find breakfast.

My bladder makes the call for me, and I decide to take a shower since I'm up anyway.

I might as well get some breakfast at the diner and work on making friends. Maybe some of the garden club will be around today.

I pad back over to my bed wrapped in my towel and stop short.

My purple dildo peeks up at me from right next to my pillow.

Beside it is the vibrator I got out in my dream.

The toys I dreamed about using. But they were firmly in their bag inside the drawer of my bedside table when I went to sleep last night. The only explanation is that I somehow pulled them out in my sleep, like a sleepwalking-type situation.

The thing is, I have never sleepwalked in my life. Why would I have started now? It doesn't make any sense. Unless...

Unless that *was* all real.

I laugh and shake my head. There's an explanation for this, there has to be, but that explanation definitely isn't my sheets actually being sentient and fucking me better than anyone ever has. I know I considered it last night, but in the warm light of morning it's just too absurd to believe. That's just not how the universe works.

It would be nice if it were, I think.

After Nick, I'm nowhere near ready to put myself out there again. I think it'll probably be a long time until I am. But I don't exactly want to give up sex, either. My toys are great, but it's nice to not have to do all the work.

Not that I got to experience that with Nick. He wanted sex constantly, but he always wanted me to do everything: dress up for him, be on top, say the exact right thing in the exact right way. And after all of that, he didn't even care if I got off.

In the early days, it happened about half the time, mostly when we were in a semi-public place and the thrill of potentially getting caught heightened the experience for me. But once the initial sex-frenzy of the early days ended, I almost never came with him.

And even when I did, it was nothing like with the sheets.

I sigh and put my toys away. My imagination is running wild again. My mom always used to tell me I should be a writer, with all the stories I'd tell myself. But anxiously worrying about things and creating whole worlds and characters are two very different things, and I'm not interested in sitting behind a computer all day.

Besides, if I wrote books that are anything like my imagination, they would be full of anxious people having bad things happen to them.

And apparently fucking their sheets.

I'm not sure there's a market for that.

When my toys are safely back in their bag I make my way downstairs, happy when the hostess at the diner sits me right by the door, where all the other diners have to walk past me to get seated.

Two hours and an omelet, a side of hash browns, three strips of bacon, a side of fruit salad, a glass of orange juice, and two cups of coffee later, I have a bunch of new numbers and plans to go out to karaoke on Friday night (I was right about there being exactly one bar, and also about the fact that that's where the entirety of Friday nightlife happens).

There are also a handful of local guys who look at me with enough interest that I know I could easily fulfill my wish of actual non-solo sex if I wanted to.

But my mind keeps drifting back to that dream.

I make a deal with myself: as long as the dreams keep me satisfied, I don't have to put myself back out there. But once the sex dreams dry up, for lack of a better phrase, I have to start dating. It seems fair.

Besides, sex dreams are usually pretty rare for me. Yeah, I've had them almost every night I've been in Newport so far, but they'll have to slow down at some point.

My phone rings as I walk out of the diner and I glance at the screen. My heart races when I see the name: *Nick*.

I send him to voicemail, but he immediately calls back. We repeat this little dance two more times before I angrily accept the call.

"What?"

"Is that any way to greet your boyfriend?" Nick asks, and he has the audacity to sound hurt.

I snort. "You're not my boyfriend. Pretty sure you gave up that title when you walked out on me seven months ago."

"Pretty sure you decided to keep that title when you decided to stay in my house. *My* house," he repeats again, stressing the word "my" to remind me that only his name was on the deed.

"Last I checked, dating someone isn't a requirement for them being your landlord." I make my way around the side of the buildings, walking through the alley and up the stairs to my apartment. As much as I want to get to know my new neighbors, this conversation probably won't make the best impression. This is definitely a conversation to have behind closed doors.

"Oh, what, you're fucking your new landlord now?" His voice drips with disdain, and a shocked laugh bubbles out of me at both his anger and the wild leap in logic he just made.

"That's none of your goddamn business." I practically growl the words, and I know it sounds defensive. Like I actually *am* fucking my new landlord. Never mind that she's old enough to be my grandmother, that I'm not into women, and that he did enough of a number on me that it'll be a while before I want to fuck *anyone* again.

Because it really isn't any of his business.

"Just like that, huh? You just...moved on?" He says this quietly, like he's hurt, and for a second I actually feel a prickle of misplaced guilt. Which is ridiculous. *He* left *me.* He didn't even have the decency to break up with me, either, he just...left. He ghosted me for seven months.

He was always like this, though. He would twist situations around until I found myself apologizing when he was actually the one in the wrong. It got to the point where I just stopped talking about anything that bothered me, because I knew it would just end up with me feeling worse, and guilty, and like *I* had done something wrong, even when it initially seemed so clear that he was the one who had.

Even when he left, I spent weeks telling myself that I must have done something to make him ghost me. I stayed up all night trying to figure out what it was, so I could apologize for the right thing and magically make him come back.

Sometime over the past seven months, I realized I was never actually the problem. He was.

Every single time.

Something dawns on me, sending a cold wave of discomfort through me. "Why did you decide to contact me now?"

"What do you mean?" He sounds too innocent.

"In your email, you said you noticed the utilities had been cancelled, but none of them were cancelled effective immediately. There's still another week until the end of the month, and that's when they run out. And they weren't in your name anyway, so you wouldn't have gotten a notification. So how did you know I wasn't at the house anymore?"

He's silent.

He only ever used to get silent like this when he realized he'd fucked up and was trying to figure out a way out of it.

"Have you been...*watching* me?" Chills race down my spine at the thought of it. Were the neighbors reporting my whereabouts to him? Did he install cameras in the house? How the hell did he know I left?

"You were living in my house. It's reasonable to keep tabs on your tenants."

"I wasn't your tenant; I was your *girlfriend*!" I explode, dropping onto my bed and putting the phone on speaker. Right now, even just holding the phone that his voice is coming out of feels like too close of contact with him.

"You're the one who said I'm not your boyfriend." I can hear his pout through the phone. And the thing is, at one point, it would have worked on me. I would have apologized and smoothed things over. But in the seven months since he ghosted me, I've gained a lot of perspective.

So I just hang up instead.

He calls me back immediately, but I let it ring out, over and over until he eventually gives up and sends me a single text.

You owe me rent for all the time you lived there for free, I'll find you and I will make you pay

Nausea floods me and I curl up on my side. I don't know if I'm scared or just exhausted by all the shit with Nick, but I kick the covers up over me and spend the rest of the day in bed, too...whatever I'm feeling to move.

I marathon small-town romance movies, and by the time I go to sleep, I'm feeling a little bit better.

CHAPTER EIGHT

Eva and Jack show up ten minutes before closing on Wednesday, and they browse until it's time for Gertie and me to close.

Once the shop is all locked up, the four of us go to the Thai restaurant that's on the farthest side of downtown. The restaurant faces a park, and on the other side of the park is a forest that apparently has nice walking trails. I'm not a big nature person, but maybe I'll check them out some time.

I'll admit I didn't have high hopes for a Thai restaurant in a town of this size, but the food is absolutely incredible. And, like everywhere else in town, it's much more affordable than I expected.

"Oh, Gertie, I meant to ask. Did you sell those sheets we found at the market a few weeks ago? I didn't see them in the store, but I wasn't sure if you'd put them out yet," Eva says around a mouthful of drunken noodles.

Gertie shakes her head. "I couldn't bear to part with them. I stuck them up in the apartment for Nikki to use."

Eva turns her gaze to me. "Aren't they gorgeous? And magical, too, if the stories the vendor told us are to be believed. She said they—" She pauses. "Never mind."

"No, what is it?" I'm curious, both because of her words and because of how her gaze darts around almost guiltily.

And because of the magic I experienced with them the other night, though I know that can't be what she's referring to.

"How do you feel about...supernatural stuff?" she asks quietly.

"Are you about to tell me my sheets are haunted?" I laugh.

But then the laugh catches in my throat.

Because if I believed in hauntings, that would actually explain a lot. I had another dream last night. Like the first night, I woke up remembering very little. But I could have sworn when I woke up that I felt the ghost of silk across my panties.

Panties that were fully on, and I woke up with my usual level of frustration, not like the night I remember in vivid detail.

The night that felt real enough that it almost makes me believe in hauntings.

"Not haunted, per say," Eva says shiftily. "Just that there are some weird stories about those sheets. Apparently they inspire...amorous connections." She blushes hard, and beside her, Jack laughs.

"Amorous connections? What is it, the 1800s?" he teases.

"Well, I can't say I'm surprised," Gertie says. "Between the silk satin and that barely-there pattern, the sheets are... well, there's really no other way to say it. Those are some damn sexy sheets."

We all laugh at those words coming out of Gertie's mouth, and the tension at the table dissolves almost instantly.

But in the back of my mind, I can't stop thinking about what Gertie said, and it's still on my mind when I climb the steps to my apartment an hour later. They *are* sexy sheets. Sexier than I will ever admit to anyone, because I understand just how batshit crazy it would make me seem.

I sit on the couch to watch a movie on my laptop, then change my mind and walk over to my bed and examine the sheets.

They're not haunted.

There's no supernatural explanation for why they "inspire amorous connections," like Eva said. They're just really nice sheets, and *if* they make people horny, well, that's just because they're so luxurious.

Right?

I mean, that has to be it.

I fold the peach-colored duvet down so it's only covering the very foot of the bed. It wasn't involved in the...activities the other night, but it's part of a set with the sheets, so if they're haunted, it probably is, too.

I run a hand along the edge of the bed, feeling the soft sheets under the pads of my fingers. They really do feel nice. The texture of the pink spots is ever so slightly different than the texture of the peach background, but it's subtle enough that I've never noticed until just now when I'm focusing all of my attention on them.

Images of these sheets tying me up fill my mind.

Pinning me to the bed, twining around my wrists and ankles. Caressing my body and even going so far as to fill me up.

Fuck, I'm getting wet just thinking about it.

I grab my two favorite toys—the ones I never got to use the other night—and stalk back to the couch.

I drop my head back and tease my entrance with the purple dildo before sliding it inside myself. But within seconds, my eyes have opened, and I'm looking back at the bed.

Because the thing is, supernatural explanation or not, real or dream, the best sexual encounter of my entire life involved those sheets. And a weird, filthy, strange-enough-that-I'm-not-going-to-examine-it, part of me wants to look at those sheets while I get myself off.

Wants to pretend those sheets are watching me back.

I want to give them a show.

I speed up, pumping the dildo in and out of my drenched pussy, gripping it with my inner walls like my life depends on it.

I'm panting. Writhing. I'm so lost in my pleasure that I almost don't notice the duvet hitting the floor and the top sheet sliding off the bed.

Satin is slippery, I tell myself. That's the whole point of using that weave on the silk. The sheets aren't *actually* moving on their own, it's just basic physics: I must have jostled the top sheet when I was running my hand along it, and it lost its grip on the fitted sheet so that it was just barely holding on, and gravity finally finished doing the work a moment ago.

But that doesn't explain why the sheet is on top of the duvet, rather than under it.

And then the sheet unmistakably moves, fully on its own accord.

I watch at it slithers across the floor, and I don't realize I'm holding my breath until it touches my foot.

I gasp. Loudly.

"What the fuck?" I ask aloud.

The sheet withdraws, like it's hurt.

Or scared.

Like it's wondering if maybe it did the wrong thing by touching me.

And somehow, amidst all the weirdness going on right now, the only thought running through my mind is *oh good, my sheets want to make sure I'm okay with being touched before they do it again. They clearly understand consent.*

Which is an objectively strange thought. But then I think about it. I felt fully awake when they fucked me, and every other night I woke up horny, not sated. And right before they made they move, I literally said I wanted to be fucked.

Did they…hear me? Did they wait until they had explicit consent before fucking me better than any man ever has?

No. That's absurd.

I laugh, thinking my horniness has fled in the face of such preposterous thoughts. But I forgot I still had a dildo inside of me, and when I laugh, my vagina clenches around it. I can feel the thick veins that rib the silicon cock inside me, and my eyes roll back a little.

Suddenly I don't care about whether this is real, or the sheets

are haunted, or what. I just need to get off, and I know the sheets
will get me there.

So I give in.

CHAPTER NINE

"Come fuck me," I whisper, looking right at the sheet on the floor in front of me.

I swear to god, it swells. Like my words have...given it an erection?

It goes back to caressing my ankle, and in my peripheral vision I think I see the corners of the fitted sheet lifting off from the bed. I don't look though; I'm too turned on by the teasing way the silk satin of the top sheet is winding its way up my leg, with just enough pressure to make me think of being tied up and pinned down.

I work the dildo in and out of me faster, but the fitted sheet reaches me and wraps itself so tightly around my wrists and thighs in one fluid motion that I can't keep maneuvering the toy in and out of me.

I moan, but the sheet only tightens.

Is it...possessive? Is this the bedding's way of saying "I don't share. If I'm not fucking you then nobody is"?

Most importantly: why do I find that so hot?

I've never been into possessive partners. I've never liked jealousy or people I'm sleeping with acting like they have some kind of ownership over my body and what I'm allowed to do with it. I've just never understood how people find that sexy.

Until now.

"Fine, then fuck me yourself," I challenge, glad my voice comes out strong and clear as I issue my challenge. "I need to get off. Now."

My words pinch off in a whine as the top sheet reaches my upper thigh and caresses me there, just out of reach of the aching throb between my legs, but it feels so good anyway.

"Tease," I murmur. The top sheet shakes, almost like it's...laughing? "I said fuck me."

The vice grip around my wrists and thighs loosens, and for a second, I think I messed up. Maybe I offended the sheets and they're done playing with me.

But then the fitted sheet snakes around my throat and pulls just tight enough to make my blood pound.

And, oh.

Oh.

They liked it.

The other night, the bedding rewarded me for submitting, but it looks like today we're playing a game of dominance, and if I keep pushing back and challenging the bedding's authority, it'll get rougher with me.

So that's exactly what I do.

"Is that all you've got?" I ask, infusing my tone with as much condescension as I can. I'm rewarded by a tightening of the silk around my throat. Blood rushes to my head. And to my clit, which throbs.

My legs are nudged apart, and I look down in time to see a thick, twisted rope of silk satin spear into me. There's nothing soft or gentle about the action, no easing its way into me to give me time to adjust. It just fills me hard and fast, and I cry out in pleasure.

The other end of the top sheet spreads out and folds itself around my ankles, pinning me more softly than its fitted counterpart, but just tight enough to promise that it can give me more if I give it a reason to.

I'm tempted.

Very, very tempted.

The sight of the same piece of cloth simultaneously fucking me and binding me is the sexiest thing I've ever seen. No man could ever fill me and pin me in place so thoroughly with nothing but his own body.

The top sheet thrusts in and out of me hard and fast, and I buck my hips against it, meeting it stroke for stroke until something shifts between us.

It's like the air grows heavy, and the sheets get gentler. The fitted sheets loosen their grip on my throat and the top sheet pumps in and out of my more slowly, like suddenly it wants to take its time worshipping my body, instead of fucking me.

I've never been worshipped before.

The sheets move almost reverently, caressing me as they gently hold me in place and fuck me so slowly it brings tears to my eyes.

The top sheet stills inside me, and there's a whisper of silk across my cheek as the fitted sheet wipes the tears from my eyes.

"I'm fine." I giggle at the absurdity of it all. "I'm fine. I'm just not used to feeling so *wanted*. I'm just realizing I've never had this before, and it's—good. It's really good. So don't stop. Please."

The sheets hesitate, as if making sure that's really what I want.

"I'm crying because it's almost too good to be true," I assure them, thrilled when the fitted sheet tightens around me ever so slightly. "I meant what I said before." I drop my voice into a purr. "I. Want. You. To. Fuck. Me."

And that's the moment when I realize there are multiple ways to worship a lover.

The top sheet caresses me slowly, softly. Reverently. It touches me so tenderly I close my eyes and take a deep, shuddering breath in response. I gasp at the slide of silk against my inner thighs. And then finally, *finally*, it starts to move inside me again.

A low keening sound fills the air, and I'm shocked to realize it's me—that *I'm* the one making that noise.

It's guttural.

Primal.

Completely unplanned and unbound and holy shit.

The bottom sheet winds its way down my arms, pinning my wrists together behind my back with just enough urgency that it sends a flood of heat between my legs.

Silk moves against me, and suddenly I find myself wrapped in silk, cradled from my shoulders to my toes in soft luxury. They turn me so I'm lying fully on the couch, and then, while I'm wrapped up, immobilized in what feels like the perfect weighted blanket only better, the sheets bring me to the brink of an orgasm.

Right as I think I'm going to tip over the edge—I'm writhing and panting and practically screaming from the pleasure—they stop.

"Please. Please don't stop. I'm so close." I'm whining, desperate, needy, and unlike with previous partners, I don't care. For once, I'm not worried about being sexy, or low-maintenance, or any of the things I've been preoccupied with in the past. I just want to come.

Silk brushes against my cheek affectionately and I lean into the feel of it. Fabric caresses my lips and I part them instinctively, moaning when it slips inside my mouth. Just enough for me to taste myself on the tip of my tongue. A breathy moan escapes me as the flavor drives my pleasure up higher.

I ride that peak for what feels like hours, the sheets not *quite* letting me come. With my wrists bound behind me I can't take matters into my own hands. I know that if I asked them to, the sheets would release me. But I don't want them to. The way they're keeping me right on the edge without allowing me relief is exquisite torture. Like they want to explore every inch of my body and wring every ounce of pleasure out of me that they can.

When they finally decide to let me come, my orgasm explodes in a screaming, gushing mess. I'm thoroughly worn out, gasping and panting as the sheets hold me tight, and it strikes me that I've never been so satisfied, so thoroughly fucked, treated with so much clear adoration as I was today.

I doze off on the couch and wake an hour before sunset, naked and sore in the most delicious way.

57

CHAPTER TEN

OKAY, so... I guess I can't keep telling myself this is a dream anymore. I was *fully* awake that whole time.

And the next three.

It's been a week since the first time I had sex with the sheets in the middle of the day. Since then, they've gotten bolder in their advances. Last night they were waiting for me when I got home. They tied me up almost the moment I walked through the door and made me come before I even had a chance to take my shoes off, laying me on the blanket on the floor, which pressed itself against my mouth to muffle my loud moans.

They've incorporated other things into the play now, too. Sometimes they'll prop a pillow underneath me, or tease me with a toy.

It's exquisite.

It's impossible.

The one thing that keeps me going is that none of the other bedding seems to be able to move on its own. Just the sheets and the duvet.

If I were having a psychotic break, I would think it would be more widespread than just the sheet set. Everything else seems normal: not just the rest of the bedding, but the rest of my life. Work is great, I've been making friends, and I have no new paranoia, besides a little about Nick making good on his threat to find me and sue me for back rent, but that seems like a reasonable worry to have.

No, the explanation for what's going on is much more unbelievable than that.

My sheets are alive.

Fully sentient.

They absolutely do *inspire amorous connections*, as Eva said. Maybe if I had a boyfriend, those amorous connections would be with him, but since I'm alone, the sheets took it upon themselves to give me pleasure.

I'm not exactly complaining.

I am, however, confused.

It's not like this makes any sense. We don't live in a world of magic and talking objects. These things aren't supposed to happen in the real world.

I push my racing thoughts aside as I walk down the steps to the store. I've started using the internal staircase; there's no reason to go all outside and all the way around the block if I can just head straight down.

I've worked half-shifts by myself, but today is my first day of handling things completely on my own from open to close. Gertie gave me strict instructions to call her if I need anything at all, even if it's just a silly question, and she said she might drop by at some point just to check on me.

It's nice having a boss who actually cares. In the past, I've been thrown into the deep end with little (or no) training, and then my bosses blamed for not knowing things they didn't teach me. In the short time I've worked for her, Gertie is already the best boss I've ever had.

I hum to myself as I get everything set up, which mostly just involves turning on the lights and unlocking the front door. I boot up the computer once the doors are open and settle in behind the counter.

The steady stream of customers slowed down over the course of last week as the novelty of my presence wore off, but I have a feeling a few people will come by to check on me on my first solo day. Not to keep tabs on me, just to make sure I'm doing okay.

Eva is the first person to show up. The bell over the door announces her as she sweeps into the shop with a wide, sunny smile.

"How's your first day working the shop alone?"

I smile. "You're the first customer. You *are* a customer, right? You didn't come in here just to loiter?" I give her a mock frown.

Eva laughs. "I absolutely came in here just to loiter. And to ask you if you want to come to the market with me on Saturday. It's about an hour and a half away, so I don't go often, but Gertie and I always find good stuff there. It's where she got your sheets, actually."

"Oh my god, yes. I definitely want to come with you."

"Great. Gertie's probably coming, too. Sorry to bring you on an outing with your boss on your day off, but I mean, it's Gertie."

"She barely counts as my boss. Or my landlord," I agree. "She's Gertie."

"Exactly." Eva peers at me across the counter. "Speaking of the sheets…you should let me set you up with someone so you can test out whether they really do inspire those amorous connections the vendor boasted about."

Something twinges inside me at the thought. A discomfort, almost like I feel guilty at the mere thought of sleeping with someone.

That's ridiculous.

They're sheets.

I can't cheat on *sheets*.

"I'm not sure I'm ready for that. Still not quite over everything that went down with my ex."

"Fair enough. But let me know when you're ready and I'll set you up with someone, okay?"

"Deal." I don't say that it'll be months, maybe even years,

before I see myself getting to that point. But when I'm finally ready, I trust her to help me find someone good.

"Maybe you can find some things for the apartment at the market," Eva suggests.

It's a great idea. I love everything Gertie furnished it with, but it's probably time to start thinking about putting some of my own stuff in there.

It's ages since I've furnished a place to my liking. Years since I've so much as bought a couch or a piece of art to hang on my walls. I haven't had a space that really felt like it was mine to decorate how I wanted since the apartment I lived in when I was eighteen. Now that I'm starting to feel more settled in Newport, I want to change that.

The thought brings tears to my eyes, and Eva thankfully turns away, letting me pretend I'm not on the verge of crying in this store.

By the time she turns back to me, my eyes are dry again.

The bell over the door jingles a little while later, and a large group spills in. There are seven of them, plus a baby, and they tell me they're on their way to an annual trip they take together every year.

Eva quietly slips out the door with a little wave, and I turn my attention to the shoppers. They look a little older than me, maybe early thirties, and they're all very enthusiastic as they shop. I sell more than I expected to, and do a little happy dance as I close the till after they leave. They paid in cash, which Gertie told me a lot of people would do, even though we take card and contactless pay.

"There's something about this town and its quiet, simple ways that makes people want to do things the old-school way. I think that's part of why this store does so well. People come in and buy old things to help them remember their time in an old town." She sighed wistfully, and I almost asked her what she was thinking about, what old things this place made her remember, but something stopped me.

I wasn't sure she was ready to have that conversation with her brand-new employee just yet. I've been here less than a month; that isn't long enough for most people to open up.

It certainly isn't long enough for me to. Even Eva and Jezelle, the only people I've really talked about Nick with, are under the impression that our relationship lasted a few months, maybe a year at most. Not multiple.

So I let Gertie keep her secrets, and I keep a few of my own.

Nick called again this morning and left a voicemail I still haven't listened to. I'm not sure I will. There's nothing that man has to say to me that I actually want to hear.

The rest of the day passes quickly, with an even mix of tourists and locals coming into the store. Most of the locals are just here to see me, but a few of them do make purchases. There are a lot of useful things here, after all. Gorgeous lamps and rugs, chests and furniture, bird cages. And it's priced very well for an antique store. I've been eyeing a few of the pieces in here for the apartment, but I haven't taken the plunge to actually buy anything yet.

It's like I've been holding my breath, unable to believe that I really get to make this apartment *mine*, but when Eva invited me to the market, my mind went wild with planning.

At the end of the day, I flip the sign to *closed* and lock the door, then wander the place, picking out the things I want for myself. I left my wallet upstairs, so I run up and grab it, yelling out to the sheets that I can't get distracted yet, just in case they're waiting for me.

They're perfectly quiet, lying on my bed as though they're just any other set of non-sentient bedding.

I run back down and pop $160.82 into the till, then haul my new finds up the stairs.

The lamp with the stained-glass shade goes next to the couch; the set of small pink glass dishes goes on my bedside table; the rocking chair and its matching rocking ottoman go in front of the window, where they'll be perfect for reading in the winter; and the three framed paintings get propped against the wall for now until I can ask Gertie if I'm allowed to put holes in the walls. Normally I wouldn't care what my landlord thinks, I'd just spackle over it before I left, but unlike with all my previous landlords, I actually like and respect Gertie.

One I've locked the door to down to the store, I turn to my bed.

"Okay, I'm all yours."

And for the rest of the night, the sheets show me exactly how true that is.

CHAPTER ELEVEN

Eva knocks on my door at six on Saturday morning. Gertie's niece is running the store today while we go to the market to source new stock with Eva.

Normally, I wouldn't have been fully awake when she arrived, but I think the sheets knew I had an early morning. They woke me up slowly and deliciously, and my body is still tingling as I slide into the back seat of the car.

The drive passes quickly with the three of us (Eva, Gertie, and me) singing along to oldies on the radio.

The market isn't what I expected. I'd never been to an antique market before, or a flea market, or honestly even a farmer's market, but there are a ton of people here. It looks like a music festival, but more permanent: the booths sit on poured concrete slabs, and there's a paved walkway that winds between them. At night, this place would be absolutely stunning, especially if they strung some fairy lights up in the trees. It honestly feels a little bit magical, and a pleasant tingle runs down my spine.

"Great, huh?" Eva grins, and I can't help but smile back. "Keep an eye out for a tent with strings of Scrabble tiles hanging in front of the opening. Like those bead curtains, but letters instead. That's the woman we bought the sheets from."

There doesn't seem to be any consistency to the types of vendors here, or even to how they're laid out; there are antiques, jewelry, various artisanal jams and condiments, and even a guy with a typewriter who'll write you a poem about the topic of your choosing. It's wild and random and so perfect it makes my heart burst. It's very different from Newport, but somehow it feels every bit as much like home.

Gertie is the first one to split off, saying there's a specific vendor she wants to try to find. Apparently the market doesn't give vendors set locations for their booth, but instead changes their spots every week, so Gertie will have to wander until she finds it. Eva and I stick together for a while longer, and she shows me her favorite vendors when we stumble across them. One of them is a woman who sells crystals, while her two young daughters sell rocks for a dollar each. I buy a rock from each of the girls while Eva browses the crystals, and I promise to display my purchases on my windowsill.

The mom mouths her thanks to me as we leave, and I smile back. I don't want kids of my own, but I babysat a lot as a teen, and the way the girls' faces lit up when I bought their rocks melted my heart.

Eva and I split up soon after that, and I linger at almost every booth, even the ones I'm pretty sure I won't buy anything at, like the medieval weapons and the local, CBD-infused honey.

After a while I realize I might not be able to find the woman who sold Gertie my sheets on my own. I might not even be able to find her with Gertie and Eva's help. Even if she's vending today, this place is massive. I think I could spend the whole day exploring and still only see a small fraction of the booths.

I'm loving being here as a shopper, as my wallet and heavy bag can attest to: aside from the rocks I also have a jar of honey, two jars of jam, a handful of stickers, a cute set of measuring spoons, and more jewelry than I'd like to admit.

But as much as I'm enjoying shopping, a part of me can't help but wonder what it would be like to *sell* here. With the amount of foot traffic here, I bet Gertie could sell the whole contents of the store in a single afternoon.

"You know—"

I jump, surprised to find Gertie beside me. I haven't seen her in...an hour, maybe? I realize I haven't checked my watch since we arrived, and my growling stomach suggests it's probably time for lunch. She smiles at me apologetically, putting a steadying hand on my arm.

"Eva and I have talked about maybe selling here one day. Looks like you may be considering the same thing, if I'm interpreting that look in your eye correctly."

My stomach growls again, and Gertie laughs at the obvious sounds of my hunger. "Let's get you fed." She leads me over to the food trucks and texts Eva, who joins us a moment later. We order loaded cheese curds, lomito tacos, and the best bacon mac and cheese I've ever had in my life.

We split up again after lunch, with plans to meet by the entrance half an hour before closing so we don't get caught in the exit traffic. That gives me three hours to explore, and it doesn't feel like enough.

Especially once I stumble across a little booth tucked away in an alcove, so set apart that I almost miss it. The fabric overheard isn't the usual plasticky tarp material, but some sort of fine tapestry, and strings of beads hang in front of it, creating an archway.

As I get closer, I see that the beads are actually Scrabble tiles.

My heart stutters.

This is it.

The place my sheets came from.

I don't even have to step inside to know it.

When I *do* step inside, my suspicions are confirmed instantly.

"Welcome." The woman sitting in the lone chair at the back of the booth smiles up at me. Then she pauses, narrowing her eyes as she takes stock of me. "Are you enjoying the sheets?" she asks knowingly.

"How—?"

She doesn't answer, just watches me, waiting for my response, which I guess is fair. She did ask me first, after all.

"They're—they're good."

"And your partner? The same level of enjoyment?"

I shake my head.

Something clouds her expression, so brief I wonder if I imagined it. But a second later, she's smiling again, her face smooth and sweet. "Ahh," she says knowingly. "No partner. Perhaps for the best."

I just nod, unsure of what to say to this woman. I wonder if she knows? I wonder if anything else she sells here also has sentient properties. I have so many questions, but they all dry out on my tongue.

"What brings you here? I presume the woman who sold you the sheets told you where you might find me."

"No. I mean, yes, she brought me here today. But she didn't sell them to me. I'm renting an apartment from her. She kept the sheets for the space."

The woman stills.

"What?" I ask. "Is there something wrong with that?"

"No." It sounds like a lie.

But just then a group of people enter the booth and have questions for her, and somehow I get shuffled out of the tent. I wait patiently at first, looking for words in the Scrabble tiles. Most of them seem to be arranged randomly, but there are a few actual words here and there: *memory; exile; love; home.*

The other shoppers finally leave, pushing past me on their way out, and I step back into the tent...only to find the vendor gone.

I sit in the lone chair to wait for her, but after ten minutes it's clear she's not coming back. The market is closing soon, and I'm about as far from the exit as it's possible to get. I'll have to come back another day. I tear a piece off the paper bag I got at the jewelry booth and write my name and number on it, with a little note asking her to call me. I tuck it underneath the till, then I duck out of the tent, shivering at the sound of the tiles clacking behind me.

Once I'm back home, I set my purchases on the little side table by the door and drop onto my bed.

"What's your deal?" I ask the sheets. "There's a whole lot more to your story than I know, and I want to discover what it is."

They don't respond.

Of course they don't. They might be sentient, but they can't talk.

They do, however, show me how happy they are that I'm back home.

A couple hours later, after two screaming orgasms and am absolutely drenched duvet, all thoughts of the vendor who sold the bedding to Gertie have completely left my mind.

CHAPTER TWELVE

THE NEXT FEW weeks pass quickly as I settle into my new routine. Nick has called me a couple more times, but I've let it go to voicemail every time, and I haven't listened to any of the messages. I've bought a couple more things from the shop, and from some of the others in town, and the apartment is starting to feel more like it's mine.

I join Gertie, Eva, and Jack for pizza and ice cream, and then I go to Eva and Jack's place for a game night with some of their friends. About half of the Garden Gals are there, including Jezelle and, unfortunately, Hazel.

"Hazel's cousin is in town," Eva says as we lay out cups and snacks. I'm full from the pizza, but the night is still young, and I know that in a few hours I'll be glad for the chips, candy, and veggies with dip that we're setting on the side table. "I haven't seen him since we were kids. He was an annoying little shit, but Hazel says he's gotten better since then. I hope she's right; otherwise, I'll have to kick him out of my home and that could get awkward."

"What's Hazel's deal?" I ask, popping a piece of ice into my mouth and crunching it, relishing in the way my lips so cold. "I can't tell if she just doesn't like me, or if she's always like that."

Eva hesitates, and Jack swoops in to answer.

"Both. She's always a bit reserved, but she seems more...standoffish...when you're around. I don't know why, but I bet she'll warm up to you the more time you two spend together."

I hope he's right. She seems fine, and it's not like the weird tension between us is really affecting things. But still, it'd be nice to be on better terms with her. Or at least to know why she doesn't like me.

Half an hour later I get my wish. The second one.

Because she walks in.

With her cousin.

Who is none other than my ex-boyfriend.

Nick.

Fuck.

I freeze with my drink halfway to my mouth, and Jack narrows his eyes at me.

"What?" He looks from me to the door, then back again. "That's Hazel's cousin. Do you know him or something?"

I shake my head. Not to say no, but just because I can't believe this is happening. "That's my ex."

"Oh, shit. Was it a bad breakup?"

I laugh. "It wasn't even a breakup. He just up and left. Fully ghosted me. Which was extra impressive, considering I was *living in his house at the time,*" I hiss.

"No," Jack breathes from beside me. "That's—"

"Diabolical," Eva finishes.

I gulp the rest of my rum and coke and slam my cup down on the side table next to me, barely noticing as the cheap, red plastic crinkles.

I stalk across the room, fuming as I go.

"What are you doing here?" I've done such a good job of keeping the details of the relationship mostly to myself, but right now I don't care who knows. I'm fuming.

"Nikki." Nick smiles at me, like he's happy to see me. But I know better. I know *him* better. I recognize that smile for what it really is: gloating that he's gotten the upper hand. "I'm just visiting my cousin, Hazel. I was shocked to find out you'd recently moved to town. I was wondering where you'd gotten to.

I'd hoped we could talk before the party, but you never answered my calls."

Shit. The voicemails. The ones I never listened to, because I didn't want to hear anything he had to say.

It's my own damn fault I'm blindsided right now. He knows it. I know it. And I can't say anything to challenge him without looking like the bad guy in front of all my new friends who don't know the story.

Fucking great.

"Can we talk?" he asks, his eyes pleading. "I've really missed you, and I just want to..." he trails off, running a hand through his perfectly coiffed wavy brown hair. "I just want to talk. See how you're doing. After you left that way, I've been worried sick."

"After *I* left?" I grit out through clenched teeth. "That's real fucking rich. But yeah, sure, let's talk. Outside." I breeze through the front door and whirl around the moment he steps out behind me and closes the door.

He just looks at me, like he's waiting for me to apologize, or grovel, or any of the things I might have done once upon a time.

But not anymore. Two can play this game now.

I glare at him.

He glares back.

"You wanted to talk," I say, dropping my voice low. "So, talk."

My words clearly take him aback, and he blinks and almost seems to sway on his feet for a second. My lips curl into a cruel smile.

"See, Nick, the thing is when you walked out on me like that, you gave me a whole lot of time to think. About our relationship, about the way you treated me. About myself. And I realized I deserved better. *Much* better. I don't have to put up with your shit anymore, so I'm not going to."

"You owe me rent."

"We never had a lease. I don't owe you shit." I cut him off the second he opens his mouth to respond. "I've talked to a lawyer, and I'm prepared to go to court, if that's where this is headed. And I'll win. At which point we'll counter-sue for court costs." It's a lie, at least the lawyer part. But I did look it up, and I will absolutely win if he does decide to be stupid enough to try to sue me for back rent. As for the counter-suit, I'm pretty sure I saw that in a movie or something. Judging by the way he goes pale, my bluff is convincing. "I have the time, and I have the money, so," I shrug, "your call."

He sputters, clearly furious that I've managed to turn this around on him. That I've bested him.

"I have to thank you, Nick. If you hadn't left the way you did, I probably would have stuck with you for the rest of my life. You were fucking terrible the whole time we dated, but you did a really good job of not crossing the lines that would have made me walk away. You were just barely good enough to make me stay. And then *you* left. You freed me. So, thanks. Friends?" I give him the most saccharine smile I can muster and breeze past him.

His hand shoots out to grab my upper arm, and I turn back to him with deadly slowness.

"There's a house full of people in there, and half of them are pressed up against those pretty bay windows, ready to bear witness to whatever you're about to do, so I'd choose your next move very carefully," I warn him.

He releases me and I walk back into the party.

For the rest of the night, I ignore him completely, doing my best to pretend he isn't there. To his credit, or maybe out of a sense of self-preservation, he ignores me back. Hazel's eyes dart between the two of us, and I wonder what he's told her about me. What lies he's spouted to make her think I was in the wrong. I'll have to clear the air with her.

It'll be tricky; she clearly likes her cousin, so I can't come out the gate too strong, or that might turn her against me more. But now that I know what her problem with me is, I have a feeling I can fix it.

I grab my cup, climb onto the coffee table, and toast to new friends and to putting the past behind us.

CHAPTER THIRTEEN

JACK WALKS me home around 2 am, as the party is winding down, and waits at the bottom of my stairs until I unlock the door (and okay, maybe I fumble with the keys a bit, because I drank…a whole lot tonight). I wave to him and call out a quiet thanks. He salutes me, but doesn't move, and I realize he's waiting until I'm safely inside to leave.

I lock the door behind me with a heavy click of the deadbolt, then double-check it just to be sure before I slide the chain lock closed. I checked behind us on the walk to make sure Nick wasn't following us, and I don't think he'd actually come here, but knowing he's in town has me on edge. Having three locks engaged on my door helps. A lot.

I kick my shoes off and stumble to my bed, not even bothering to change out of my clothes before I drop onto my bed.

The sheets wrap around me, a soft glide of silk across my skin. I'm about to tell them that I'm not up for anything sexual tonight when I realize that doesn't seem to be their intention. Unlike most nights, they don't move between my legs, or caress my nipples, or tug at my clothes to encourage me to pull them off; the sheets just hold me, with the duvet cocooning us all.

I've always loved curling up in bed at the end of a long day, but tonight is different. This isn't me using the time alone to rest and recharge; the bedding is comforting me, holding me close, the way a partner might let you curl up in their lap and cry. Only I don't have to worry about getting my tears and snot on a partner's shirt, or whether they're sitting in an uncomfortable position. There are absolutely no considerations for my partner's needs, I can just focus fully on my own, and the realization breaks a dam within me.

I curl into a ball and sob. For the years I wasted with Nick. For the fact that for this one night, he poisoned this town that felt so safe.

One of the sheets slides out from the cocoon, disappearing off the bed, but I'm too distraught to look to see where it's going. A few seconds later the tv turns on and a small-town romance movie starts playing.

I roll over so I can see the tv, and nestle deeper into my next of sheets and blanket.

I drift off around the time the girl from the big city and the guy who runs the local post-office kiss for the first time, right before everything goes wrong for them. It's one of my favorite movies, and that night I dream about the town in the movie. It's a sweet, gentle dream, and for once I don't wake up with an ache between my thighs. The sheets inspire no amorous connections tonight. Just comfort and safety.

I wake up with puffy eyes and a splitting headache: my first hangover in years. I drag myself next door and grimace at Anya when she asks what I want.

"Oh. Gotcha. One hangover cure, coming right up." She slides a greasy egg and sausage puff pastry my way, as well as a strong coffee with whipped coconut crème on top. It's more than I usually pay for my breakfasts here, but within ten minutes I'm already feeling slightly better.

Until I see Nick walk past the café.

Thankfully he's looking straight ahead and doesn't notice me through the window, but the moment I see him I tense, and it takes everything in me not to go hide behind the counter at Anya's feet, or run out onto the sidewalk to confront him.

My one bit of comfort is that he looks every bit as miserable as I feel. The circles under his eyes are so dark they almost look like bruises, and from the way he's squinting even though it's overcast, I wouldn't be surprised if his headache is worse than mine.

Hazel walks a step behind him, and she *does* see me consuming my hangover remedy like a gremlin. Her steps falter as she scowls at me, and I glare back until she hurries to catch up with Nick.

I give it another ten minutes to make sure they're gone before slipping back upstairs to my apartment.

Today is going to be a *stay in bed and watch comfort movies* day, for sure.

I strip the sheets and duvet from the bed and bring them to the couch. They immediately wrap themselves me, the duvet providing fluffy comfort as the sheets slowly move back and forth against my skin, idly rubbing my arm while we settle in for a long day of movie marathons. I only take one break, to order and go pick up a pizza, which serves as both my lunch and dinner.

It's the kind of lazy afternoon I've always wanted to have with a partner, but none of my exes ever seemed interested. And this is somehow better than I ever imagined it would be.

Thoughts of Nick fade as the hangover does, and by the time night falls I'm determined to put that man behind me. I'll avoid him for however long he stays in town, and then that's it. I block his number and his email, so he can't get through to me anymore. There's no reason for Nick to contact me ever again, and I'm certainly not going to make it easy for him if he decides otherwise.

Through it all, the sheets hold me. Gently, tenderly, reminding me that they're here and that I deserve softness and love. It's a lesson it's taken me over twenty years to learn, and I'm so thankful to these peach and pink sheets with embroidered flowers for being the ones to make sure I knew my own worth and the depth of the love I deserve.

CHAPTER FOURTEEN

Hazel and I talk later that week, after Nick leaves town. She clearly didn't want to, but Jezelle convinced her. The two of us sit on a bench in the park, with coffees from the cafe, and I tell her everything. About how the relationship dragged on, how I lost myself, how he was never actively terrible in ways I was conscious of but made did tons of things that me shrink into myself until I felt like I'd lost myself over time. How he left without a single word and didn't deign to contact me until after I moved out.

At first, she doesn't believe me. But I show her some of our old texts, and it's impossible not to see what was going on. I wonder how I missed it while we were together. She gasps a few times reading it, and I almost feel bad for being the one to expose his true nature to her. I know he's her family, but she needs to know what he's really like.

By the time I get to the end of the story, she's fuming.

"I'm sorry I believed him," she said. "That's not what he's like with me. And I'm sorry for my part in it. I told him you'd moved to town. I knew who you were the moment I saw you, and he'd told me *you* left *him* because you said his life was too small for you. So when you showed up in this tiny town, I was mad on his behalf, and I texted him. I'm so sorry. For that, and for how he treated you all that time."

I shrug. "I mean, it wasn't awful, or anything." Even though the pit in my stomach whenever I think about him suggests otherwise.

"It was," she says quietly.

We leave it at that.

She and the other Garden Gals come over that afternoon. We go through about half a joint each, eat at least our weight in snacks, and watch two movies we frankly don't pay any attention to because we're all a little high and keep getting sidetracked with conversations.

It's perfect.

It's also the first time I've had anyone but Jack and Eva over to the apartment, and there's a part of me that holds my breath, waiting for something to happen. For the sheets to move, or the Gals to get *amorous*, as Eva would say.

But it all goes off without a hitch, and I breathe a sigh of relief when I close the door behind them.

It becomes a new routine: the Garden Gals and I rotate houses each Sunday (I sometimes have to join late or leave early depending on my work schedule; Gertie still works some on weekends); I see Eva and Jack at least once a week, usually on Thursdays; and I'm starting to make other friends, too. Fridays I'm usually at the one bar in town doing karaoke. I've fully settled into my life in Newport and left everything else behind.

Eva, Gertie, and I try to get to the market at least every couple of months. I always look for the woman who sold Gertie the sheets. I don't always find her tent, but when I do, I walk away remembering very little of our conversations. There's an air of mystery around her, and I can't help but think it has something to do with the sentience of the sheets, like whatever magic made that happen is cloaking her identity. I bet I'll never get answers there, but I'm not sure I feel a need to.

The important thing isn't how my sheets became sentient; the important thing is that they still treat me with the care, reverence, and lewdness that I want from them.

I've just closed the door to my apartment after the Garden Gals leave one Sunday when I feel silk wrap around my midsection.

"Biding your time until you could get me alone?" I ask, laughing into my now-empty apartment.

It doesn't feel strange to talk to the sheets anymore. Not after almost a year of this. It's just a fact of life now, and it's one I honestly can't imagine my life without anymore. It's funny how quickly, and how drastically, things can change.

I giggle as the top sheet slides along my stomach, under my dress. I'm not quite high but pleasantly buzzed, and I don't know what it is about weed, but it always makes me a little bit wet. Not even horny, necessarily, at least not emotionally. Just...ready.

Tonight, the sheets take advantage of that fact, pulling my underwear down in one smooth motion, then skipping the foreplay they usually give me and going straight for a good, hard fucking right there against the door. A part of me expected things to slow down after a while like they always do with relationships. Every partner I've ever had before got less interested in my pleasure as time went on. Not the sheets, though. Even after all these months, they're still just as tender and loving (or rough and desperate, depending on our mood) as they were at the beginning.

After a minute or so of fucking me pinned against the door, the sheets apply pressure to my clit, and I'm seconds away from coming when a knock sounds at the door.

Inches from my face.

I freeze with my mouth open in a gasp that was seconds away from turning into a scream.

The top sheet goes still inside me, and the fitted sheet loosens its grip on my ankles where it's holding them spread apart, but I don't react as quickly.

I'm panting too hard to be able to speak normally. I give myself a few seconds for my heart rate to slow and the silk slides out of my drenched core.

I take a moment to collect myself, kicking my underwear to the side and smoothing my dress back in place.

"Who is it?" I call out.

"Leah! I forgot my phone."

"Just a minute, let me grab it!" I run over to the couch and sure enough, there it is, all pink and sparkly on the coffee table.

I fling the door open, harder than I mean to, and Leah's eyes go wide at the sight of me as I shove her phone into her hands.

"Do you have a man in there?" She whispers. "We literally *just* left, was he waiting?"

"What? No!" My voice is high and shrill, even to my own ears. It sounds like I'm lying.

There *isn't* a man in here, though. The truth is so much stranger. Even though I've gotten to knew her and the rest of the group pretty well over the past few months, I don't think she'd believe me if I told her what's really going on.

Weirdly, the Garden Gal I think would be most likely to believe it is Hazel. It took a while for our friendship to evolve, but now she's one of the people I'm closest with in town.

I think Eva and maybe even Gertie would understand, too.

But I have no plans to have this conversation with *any* of them.

"I'll let you get back to it," she whispers with a twinkle in her eye. "I'm going to require details, though." She wiggles her phone at me and I groan, knowing I must be blushing like crazy.

"There's nobody here," I protest.

"Mmhmm. Sure." Her eyes slide past me and land on the floor.

On the sheets.

Dread pools in my stomach.

"That's why you suddenly need to do laundry, because there's nobody in there? Or was it just solo time? There's no shame in that. Honestly, weed makes me weirdly horny, I'm about to go have some solo time of my own. Bye!" She winks and descends the stairs, and I sink against the door.

That was too close for comfort.

"I probably should wash you soon, huh?"

Every time I do it, I feel guilty, like maybe I'll drown them if I stick them in the washer. They clearly have emotions and can physically feel things, and I don't know how they feel about going through the wash. And it's not exactly like I can ask them about it. They're sentient, but it's not like they can *talk*.

An idea strikes me.

"Should I wash you? Give me an orgasm right now if the answer is yes."

Both sheets surge up from the floor, working me hard and fast, and I come within seconds, immediately finding the orgasm that faded so quickly when Leah knocked on the door.

Well, then. That settles it.

It's time to wash my magical fucking sheets.

"But first," I say, pulling my dress over my head, "I think I need to come again."

ACKNOWLEDGMENTS

Bedding the Bedding is my first ever sentient object romance (though by the time it publishes I will have already written the next two). It's the first in what I hope becomes a long list of titles under this name/in this genre.

When I picked up the first sentient object book I ever read, I went into it expecting silly fun—and it absolutely delivered on that front, but I wasn't expecting the amount of heart in it. I'm not claiming that my own books are super groundbreaking or anything, but many of the books I've read in this genre blend the funny and absurd with some really powerful emotional journeys, social commentary, and other elements that make them really resonate with a lot of people.

So for this series, that's what you can expect. Silly smut with a hefty dose of a character journey for the MC. Don't get me wrong, you can probably expect some stories from me in the future that are purely silly bullshit fun, because those stories absolutely have a place, and I've personally clung to those types of stories as a lifeline.

In the meantime, if this is your first sentient object romance (and even if it's not), I recommend looking into some of the other authors writing in this genre. Whether you're looking for silly fun, titillation, emotional journeys, or social commentary (or some blend of those), I can pretty much guarantee there's someone writing what you're looking for.

Now, onto the acknowledgements. I'm lucky to be surrounded by a lot of amazing authors who have supported me on this new venture, whether they're interested in sentient object romance or not.

I'd like to especially thank my incredible beta readers Carrie, Kristin, and Angel. Thank you for being down to read a book about sexy sheets, and for approaching this read with as much care and thoughtfulness as you do everything else.

To Bailey, for the blurbs. I don't know what I would have done without you.

Leslie, Molly, and Amy, thanks for all the time you spent brainstorming, listening to my wild ideas, and generally supporting me.

Finally, thanks to bi+ book gang for the writing sprints that kept me going, and the cottage for all the support as I branched out into a new genre. Thanks for holding my hand and cheering me on and coming along for the ride. I will always and forever appreciate y'all.

ALSO BY ANNARA LAYNE

A SNEAK PEEK AT
PLOWING THE PLOW

Author's note: I debated whether to use a spicy scene or the opening chapter here, and I ultimately settled on the first spicy scene. it's a few chapters into the book, so you may be missing some context. It's also not the final version, so it may look a little different in the book itself.

I wake up the next morning feeling completely refreshed. It's rare for this to happen after a flare—usually it takes a few days for me to get back to my baseline. But I feel good enough to walk around the property. Assuming I *do* stay, which definitely isn't certain yet, I'll need to decide what to do with the property. My parents hired workers to help them, but I'm not sure I'll be able to afford the amount of work this place will need, especially since my parents were able to work the land themselves, and I'd need to hire two extra laborers to account for that.

I pop in my headphones and sling my old bag over my shoulder. I don't bother to clear out any of the contents—a red flare, a notebook and pencil, a box of condoms that's probably long expired—and throw in a couple granola bars and a bottle of water. I set off, listening to an audiobook as I walk the acres of land that I grew up on, trying to imagine selling it off. There are a few people in town who might want to take a field or two off my hands, and sometimes people will move here specifically to start up a farm. But I'm not thrilled about either option; if I'm going to keep the farm, I want to keep *all* of it.

I let myself just feel the land as I listen to my book. It's the newest romance by my favorite author, Gabriella Henriquez. I was on the waitlist at the library for three months, even though I requested it before its release. They had more copies of the ebook, but sometimes even holding an e-reader can put a bit too much strain on my wrists, or craning my neck to look down at it can hurt my neck and shoulders too much.

E-readers tend to work better for me than paperbacks (or hardcovers, which I can't do at all), but I tend to stick to audiobooks just so I don't have to worry about it. There's nothing worse than getting to a particularly good part in a book and having to set it down because my body won't cooperate; audiobooks don't have that issue for me.

This book is starts with the characters meeting each other on a wild night out. Mason, the male main character, gets broken up with over text while he's picking out lingerie for his (now-ex) girlfriend. Iliana, the female main character, happens to be right next to him, picking out something for a spicy scavenger hunt run by the sex club she's a member of, when it happens. They team up for a night of tipsily running around the city to check things off her list, and then finally end up at his hotel together at dawn.

I reach the creek behind the property right as the door to the hotel room closes behind them and he drops to his knees in front of her the second the door is locked.

"Fuck, Mason, I want you so bad."

Mason grins up at me from between my legs. I can feel his breath against the most sensitive part of me and I press my hips toward him in a silent plea for more.

"Greedy girl." He chuckles, and the sound sends molten fire through me.

"Mason," I whine. If this were anyone else, I'd be embarrassed by how needy I'm being. But I'm never going to see this man again after tonight, and that gives me the freedom to be as bold an uninhibited as I've always wanted to be.

Before I can say anything more, Mason's mouth is on me, hot and wet against the thin scrap of lace we picked out together when we met.

This is my favorite part of any smutty book, when the tension that's been building finally breaks. Sometimes the later sex scenes are better for the characters—and they're often objectively more exciting, because the characters are comfortable enough to know, and ask for, exactly what they want. But there's something about that first time the tension breaks, where we get that insight into the characters' minds for the first time, and we learn this new side of them, that I just love.

What anatomy words do they use? Are their moans breathy or lewd? Do they ask for exactly what they want or do they wait to let their partner explore first?

It's these scenes that are the reason I started writing, something only Jensen knows about me. It's not like I've ever published anything, and I don't expect to do much writing while I'm here.

I'm normally the kind of person who can listen to any level of smut in public with a straight face but I don't know what it is about Gabriella Henriquez…she gets me blushing *hard*. And she exclusively hires actual sex workers to voice the audiobooks—people who professionally record audio porn. So the sex scenes are truly next-level.

I learned with her first book that I can only read them when I am alone.

In my own home.

And preferably already in bed.

For a second I think about pausing the book until I'm back in my room and can do something about the throbbing between my legs and the wetness that I know is spreading there…but then I realize I'm completely alone out here. The nearest neighbors are half a mile, a patch of dense forest, and an electric fence away. There's nobody to see me if just slip my hand into my underwear and get myself off alongside the characters.

I shouldn't do that, right?

But the more I think about it, the more I realize there's no concrete reason not to.

I've never masturbated outside before. I've had sex in fields—what person in farm country hasn't—but somehow this feels so much more vulnerable than that.

Plus, it's broad daylight. If someone saw me from half a field away, they'd know exactly what I'm doing.

Still, I'm in a secluded enough spot that nobody's going to accidentally see me—they'd have to walk through a whole field, round a bend, go through a small copse of trees, and then make it halfway through the field I'm in before they'd likely even know I'm out here.

And the flip side of them being able to see me from half a field away is that I'd be able to see them, too; I'd see them coming long before they ever actually… saw me *coming*.

As Mason pulls Iliana's panties down with his teeth, I shimmy my own pants off and then lie back in the field. The grass is high and scratchy enough that I consider going inside. Bed sheets would be much nicer against my skin than unkempt grass.

But then Mason groans against Iliana's sweet cunt (the author's words, not mine), and I know I won't make it back to my room. I need to get off.

Now.

I play with myself over my underwear, rubbing and teasing my clit through the soaked cotton. The feeling of the wet fabric against my fingers turns me on more, especially with all the descriptions of *wet* in the book.

Mason sucks Iliana's clit then slowly pushes his tongue inside her. He fucks her with his tongue, thrusting hard and fast, and I don't even try to hold back my moan. I'm not in an apartment with thins walls and nosy neighbor; I can be as loud as I want to be.

The thought sends a bolt of heat right to my clit.

I slip a finger inside myself in time with the how I imagine Mason's tongue. In and out, slowly at first but picking up speed as the narration gets faster.

I circle my thumb with my clit while I thrust my fingers inside myself, and it feels so good I know I won't last much longer. The way Mason is drawing out Iliana's orgasm, I might come before her.

I'm panting and barely touching my clit by the time he finally rolls a condom on and slips inside her. I know the orgasm scene is going to be worth waiting for so I can have my own at the same time.

He finally lets her come, thanking her for the privilege while his tongue is still inside of her.

I scream out, my own cunt pulsing around my fingers and I'm wracked by the most powerful orgasm I've had in a long time.

The chapter ends with her orgasm while Mason stands and grabs a condom from his wallet. I pause the book to catch my breath. The characters aren't done yet, and neither am I.

With my headphones silent, I think I hear something. It's probably just an animal or something, but just to be sure I sit up and look in the direction of the sound.

There's nobody in the field.

What there is, however, is the plow.

It trundles toward me, churning up the dirt as it goes.

With nobody behind it.

That can't be right.

There are plows out there that are self-propelling, but they still need someone to be there to keep an eye on them. But this plow is over a hundred years old. It's frankly a miracle the blade is still sharp and the handle unbroken; self-propelling is a far-away fantasy.

And yet, there it is, moving on its own.

And look. The thing is, I grew up in Appalachia, in the shadow of the mountains that watched over me my whole life. I grew up on stories of impossible things. Cryptids, strange sightings, phenomena that can't be explained.

Something is propelling this plow.

It isn't a battery. It's not a person, I can see that plain enough from here.

But the fact that the plow is working the field instead of, I don't know, going haywire or attacking me or just refusing to budge when it's pushed, means whatever force is behind it likely isn't malevolent.

I mean, it's being *helpful*. There's no evil spirit I can think of that would take its time plowing a field.

Honestly, if this were happening any other time I'd probably get up to examine it, or run home and make Jensen and Cole come to check it out.

But I'm right in the middle of the first sex scene in a Gabriella Henriquez book so frankly I have more important things on my mind. The mystery of the plow is just going to have to wait.

I close my eyes and press play on the audiobook, shivering at the sound of the male narrator's voice as it switched to Mason's point of view.

Sliding into Iliana inch by inch feels like coming home.

Her eyes widen, but I only see them for a second before slamming my own shut. She feels so good, so hot and wet and tight that if I'm not careful, I'll come within seconds. When I'm fully seated inside her, I take a deep breath, letting myself adjust to the feeling of her. She feels so fucking good. There's nowhere in the world I'd rather be—and that includes the place I'm supposed to be right now. But fuck the consequences of missing that meeting; missing this moment with Iliana would be infinitely worse.

A squeaking sound right next to me makes me open my eyes, and I jump a little at how close the plow has gotten. It's right in front of me, practically between my legs.

Kind of like how Mason is positioned in front of Iliana. I can't help but be a little turned on at the thought.

I look up at it as I keep fingerfucking myself. From this angle, most of what I can see is the handle, which is looking...a lot more phallic than it should.

I'm tempted...

But no. I can't put that inside me. It would be unsanitary.

But now that I've had the thought, I can't stop thinking about it. I close my eyes and try to focus on the book, but instead of picturing Mason and Iliana, the image that comes to mind is of me and the plow.

That smooth handle sliding in and out of me.

Me clenching around it as I get closer and closer to the edge.

I pause the book. I'm barely listening to it at this point anyway.

I spread my legs wider, giving the plow a better view of my fingers dipping in and out of me. My pleasure builds with every pump, until I'm writhing and panting.

But I can't quite tip over the edge.

In front of me, the plow rocks back and forth slightly, almost like when a man flexes his hips in anticipation. I bite my lip, wishing there was a way I could fuck the plow. I'm desperate to feel it inside me. But even in my haze of lust, I'm still thinking clearly enough to know better than to shove a dirty piece of wood inside myself.

That's when I remember the condoms in my bag. They're old, but likely still within their expiration date. The chances of them breaking are low. And I'm too turned on to care much about that infinitesimal chance.

I sit up, grab a condom from the box, and unwrap it.

Then I pause.

If this is some weird supernatural thing going on (I do snort at that *if*), maybe I should check in with the plow. I'm not really sure how to get consent from a sentient object, but if it can move on its own, there's clearly some sort of thought process or feeling behind it—or whatever is possessing it. And it should be able to give me some indication of whether it's interested in fucking me.

"Do you..." I pause.

"Is this—" I can't help the giggle that bursts from my mouth. This is hands down the weirdest experience of my life, and talking to the plow out loud makes that harder to ignore.

It's a plow! A literal, actual plow!

A plow you're trying to plow, a voice in the back of my mind says. The thought makes me laugh harder, but I'm way too horny to get distracted for long.

It takes a few minutes for me to get myself under control.

Those minutes do nothing to cool my lust. My clit throbs and my fingers are still slick with my own arousal, and my nipples are so hard they almost hurt.

By the time I've pulled myself together enough to ask my question, my voice is low and husky with need.

"Do you want to fuck me?" I feel ridiculous, but as soon as I ask the question, the plow moves closer to me and tips toward me, in a move that's clearly offering me the handle.

Okay, then. That is some clear nonverbal consent right there.

And considering I'm about to fuck a *plow*, nonverbal consent is the only kind possible.

My hands shake with anticipation as I roll the condom over the smooth wooden handle of my favorite farming implement. It's been years since I've pushed this plow through the fields, but the handle feels good in my hand, like it was made to fit into it.

Which, of course, makes me wonder how well it'll fit other places.

The handle is a softer wood than you'd expect a plow handle to be, and it's been oiled well over the course of its life. It's perfectly smooth, with no knots or dry spots, and aside from the grain, the color is almost perfectly uniform. It's girthier than my favorite dildo, but I've taken bigger.

I think.

Either way, its size excites me.

"How do we..." I trail off. It's not like the plow can respond.

Not verbally, anyway.

But just like before, the plow makes clear *exactly* what it wants from me.

It tips even further forward, until the handle trails down my body slowly. Sensually. The way a lover might trail their fingers or their tongue down your stomach, slowly building the tension until you beg for them to please finally fuck you. Honestly, the lube from the condom almost makes it feel like a tongue.

The handle slides down until it's nestled right up against my soaking wet underwear, then it nudges at me as if to say *take these off.*

I shimmy them off and toss them to the side, then shift to get the handle back to where it was before.

The plow notches itself at my entrance and I gasp at the fullness of it before it's even actually inside.

"Fuck me," I whisper. My voice comes out ragged, the command more like a plea.

Then the plow pushes forward, filling me perfectly.

I moan louder than I ever have in my life. For the first time, the sound that comes out of my is something that could be categorized as a scream.

It pauses like it's checking in with me, making sure this feels good and I still want this.

It feels *so* good. Nothing in the world could make me change my mind now. Someone could walk into this field right now and I still wouldn't want to stop, that's how good it feels.

I raise my hips. The angle pushes me further down the handle as the plow pushes forward. The result is a level of fullness I've never felt before as it bottoms out inside me. I can feel the slight flare at the base of the handle as it settles against my entrance, that light lip pressing against my clit.

It pulls back out slowly, and my inner walls clench around it as the widest part slides out of me. I gasp at the sensation, and immediately rock my hips forward, desperately wanting it back inside me—but it doesn't give in.

Instead, it caresses my thigh, spreading my own slick wetness along my skin. It teases me gently, kneading my inner thighs, lightly brushing against my clit, teasing at my entrance but not fully entering me.

My pleasure builds until I'm begging, and still, it continues to play with me. As if it knows exactly how much I love to be denied my pleasure. As if it knows that getting me this desperate before finally fucking me is how I want my partners to treat me.

I've been to a lot of kink parties in the city—I've found that people in the kink scene tend to be better communicators around sex, and they do a better job overall of treating my body with the extra level of care that it needs. Even if they don't understand my disability, they understand that when I draw a boundary, it's non-negotiable. The plow somehow gives me that same level of care, despite not having prehensile thumbs or a frontal cortex.

When it finally—*finally*—enters me again, it fucks into me slow and gentle, clearly not wanting to risk hurting me.

Which I appreciate. But also, right now I want it hard and fast.

It's teased me for long enough; now I need it to be rough and messy.

"Harder," I tell it. In this position, there's not much harm my body is likely to do to itself.

The plow keeps the thrusts slow and gentle, ignoring my demand. But I want more. *Need* more.

"Harder," I demand again, pushing my hips upward, meeting its thrusts and pushing it deeper. I moan as it hits my cervix, something I always thought sounded unpleasant when I've read it in books but fuck it feels so good, just the right kind of ache. "Just like that. Please. Fuck." My words are garbled and messy as my hips keep rocking almost on their own. "Please," I whine again.

That seems to be the key to getting the plow to believe that I really can take more. The change is slow, not the fast switch-up you often get with human partners, and the progression of the thrusts deepening and speeding up heightens my pleasure in a really delicious way.

I moan again, and the sound is more lewd than any sound I've ever made before.

It honestly even turns *me* on a little bit.

More than a little bit, if I'm being honest.

"Oh fuck," I gasp. "Fuck, just like that."

Normally when I say that to a man, he immediately changes things up. A fair number of woman do, too.

But not the plow.

It fucks me the way I've always wanted to be fucked. Hard and deep—but tenderly. The plow responds to my every gasp and moan, and it doesn't take long for my legs to tense as my orgasm builds within me.

When it finally hits I scream out into the empty field, my voice raw as wave after wave of pleasure courses through me.

The plow stays inside me as I come down from the peak, and the last thing I'm aware of as I drift off is a dull ache of pleasure as it slides out of me and a quiet squeak as it trundles away.

www.ingramcontent.com/pod-product-compliance
Lightning Source LLC
Chambersburg PA
CBHW020120310726
48970CB00002B/716